VAMPIRES & VERSES

A LIBRARY WITCH MYSTERY

ELLE ADAMS

This book was written, produced and edited in the UK, where some spelling, grammar and word usage will vary from US English.

Copyright © 2022 Elle Adams
All rights reserved.

To be notified when Elle Adams's next book is released, sign up to her author newsletter.

1

"You can only win one cuddly dragon! Only one!" My cousin Estelle's voice drifted above the general chatter of the seafront as my two aunts and I made our way towards the pier.

The summer carnival my cousin presided over had drawn quite the crowd, and the collective sound of laughter and shouting almost drowned out the patter of raindrops. The summer heat wave was officially over, but even the gloomy weather wasn't enough to deter people from flocking to the pier, both from the town of Ivory Beach and from outside of it.

Crowds of academy students sat on the sandy slopes eating ice creams while families watched their kids ride the various attractions that filled every inch of the wooden pier that extended across the sand and into the sea. Running parallel to the beach were various stalls selling ice cream and snacks. I spotted Estelle's curly red hair next to a stall that offered passers-by a shot at winning a cuddly toy dragon if they could successfully throw three balls into three baskets without using magic.

"Hey, Rory!" She waved at me, her expression cheery despite the rainwater dampening her red curls and running in rivulets down her face. Her silver-lined blue cloak was embossed with our family crest of an owl sitting atop a pair of crossed wands, an indication that the library was sponsoring this event. Since our family's library was closed on Sundays, we'd all been looking forwards to helping Estelle with the grand opening, but an outbreak of book-wyrms in the history section this morning had meant Estelle had had to come to the pier alone while the rest of us dealt with the unwelcome infestation.

"Hey, Estelle." I sidestepped a group of chattering tourists and joined her next to the display of cuddly dragons. "Good turnout. Looks like most of the town's here."

"Except the vampires," said Estelle. "But that's to be expected. It's too bright and noisy for them."

"That, and they sleep during the day." My best friend, Laney, was the only inhabitant of the library who hadn't come to join in the fun, though the sun was hidden behind a thick layer of clouds and the stiff breeze from the coast was doing its best to break the illusion that it was still summer. That was August in England for you.

Aunt Candace came bounding over, clutching a giant ice cream in her hand. "Your Reaper boyfriend isn't here, either, Rory."

"I'm aware of that," I said. "He said his boss told him not to come, unless—"

"Unless someone dies," finished Aunt Candace with her usual morbidity. "I bet the Grim Reaper is secretly a fan of carnival rides. He'll show up after dark."

"No, he won't," Aunt Adelaide told her sister. "The Reaper being absent means there's no trouble, which is a good thing. No offence, Rory."

"None taken." I might be dating the town's only Reaper apprentice, but that didn't mean I was unaware that most people didn't want to see an angel of death wandering around the summer carnival.

Aunt Candace tutted. She liked a little mayhem, especially when she wasn't directly involved, but this event was Estelle's pride and joy, and I didn't want anything to ruin it. I'd already had to stop Cass from smuggling a pair of bookwyrms up to the Magical Creatures Division in the hopes of breeding her own colony.

"I wouldn't speak too soon," Cass now said from behind her mother, who'd dragged her out of the library under duress. Cass was tall and thin, like me, and she'd pulled her hood up over her red curls and buried her hands in her pockets. Coupled with her sour expression, she looked as out of place among the general cheeriness as the average Reaper.

Aunt Candace shot her a grin. "Why, do you think the vampires and Grim Reaper will *both* show up to the carnival after dark? That might be fun. Imagine if they both wanted to ride the carousel at the same time."

Cass scowled and strode past without answering, her cloak billowing behind her. She had her own hang-ups concerning the vampires, though considering we had a vampire living in the library itself—two, in fact, if you counted the slumbering one in the basement—it was understandably hard to avoid them. Weirdly enough, Cass seemed to have grown *less* tolerant of our nocturnal guest the longer she stayed in the library, and she made no secret of the fact that she thought Laney ought to live with the other vampires instead.

Never mind that it was partly our family's fault that Laney had ended up in that state to begin with. Or mine, anyway, because I'd refused to surrender my dad's journal to the group of vampires known as the Founders. That incident had led to my discovery of the hidden magical world my dad had once been a part of, and the Founders' determination to seize the journal had led to my best friend being inducted into the paranormal world as well as becoming one of the living dead.

I'd also ended up in the unenviable position of owing a favour to Evangeline, the formidable and terrifying leader of the town's vampires. Even Aunt Candace wouldn't dare make jokes about her if she were present, though admittedly, the mental image of Evangeline bickering with the Grim Reaper over who was first in line to ride the carousel was kind of hilarious.

I didn't need to encourage her, so I held my tongue and watched Aunt Candace make a beeline for the bumper cars. Upon spotting one that resembled a giant green dragon, she flagged down the pimply teenager in charge of the ride.

"Honestly." Estelle ran to intercept her, but since Aunt Candace had already climbed into the bumper car, she and I had no choice but to watch. "She can't drive, Rory. This is going to be a disaster."

Sure enough, within a minute, Aunt Candace's erratic driving had caused a pileup of no fewer than six cars stacked against the side of the racetrack.

"I can guess why she doesn't have a driving licence," I remarked to Estelle. "Sorry. I shouldn't have told her we were coming. I assumed she'd want to avoid the crowds and say no."

"It's fine," Estelle said. "I've had to break up three duels over the bumper cars today already, so this is nothing. I'm starting to think I should have hired more staff. Or put a cap on attendees."

"Hey, it's all good publicity for the library."

At that moment, a commotion arose from farther down the pier, and the wail of a child hit my eardrums, followed by several adults shouting at one another.

Estelle groaned. "Not again."

"What's going on?"

I hurried after her towards the carousel at the far end of the pier where a kid of around four or five had attached herself like a limpet to the side of a mechanical unicorn and refused to move.

"That kid has been on the ride literally all day," she said in an undertone. "The parents keep buying more tickets. I'm surprised they haven't run out of cash yet. Or maybe they have."

By the looks of things, she'd guessed right, and the kid's tantrum was due to her finally being hauled away. A frizzy-haired witch who was presumably the child's mother was engaged in a shouting match with the terrified-looking elf in charge of the carousel. The ride had stopped in its tracks, and some of the other children were starting to raise a fuss too.

Estelle walked over to them and spoke to the red-faced witch. They argued back and forth for a minute before Estelle returned to my side. "She seems to think the ride will wait for her to get some more cash before it starts again."

"Doesn't the ride only last a minute anyway?"

"Exactly." She blew out a breath. "I told her that, and she told me I'd ruined her child's day."

"Unbelievable." I took a step back as a hulking shifter came marching past and right up to the carousel, at which point the child detached herself from the unicorn and instead latched on to his arm. Was he the child's father? I'd wager he was, though the red-haired witch promptly began yelling at him when he carried their kid away from the ride.

He ignored her shouting, though the child started wailing even louder when the ride started up again.

"We'd better go." Estelle began to lead the way back to the bumper cars. "See what I mean about needing more staff?"

"You'd need one just to supervise Aunt Candace." I watched her clamber out of the dragon-shaped bumper car and abandon it on the tracks, leaving a gaggle of disgruntled tourists behind her.

"That was fun," she said, bounding over to us. "What shall I try next? Ah, there's a carousel!"

"You're too old," I told her.

"Everyone's a child at heart," she said. "Except possibly Cass."

"Where is she?" While we'd been at the carousel, my cousin had slunk away, which was typical. Granted, Cass made the term 'antisocial' look like an understatement, but Aunt Adelaide had explicitly told her to stay out of the library.

"We'll find her." Estelle led the way off the pier, only to be forced to a halt by another commotion.

Next to the pier, the burly shifter who we'd assumed was the screaming kid's father appeared to be having a tug-of-war with a stall owner over a giant stuffed red dragon. "That's mine!"

"Whoa." Estelle hurried over to them. "What's going on here?"

"He cheated!" protested the rat shifter behind the stall. "This is the fifth toy he's won today. I'm going to run out of stock."

Now that I looked, the stall did look a little sparse, with

only three dragons hanging from its wooden frame. The rest were in the arms of the same kid who'd been clinging to the merry-go-round, whose mother was nowhere to be seen.

"I'm not cheating." The large shifter refused to let go of his prize, but if he wasn't careful, he'd rip the cuddly toy clean in two. Behind him, the child let out a wail. "Now look what you did. You made her cry."

Estelle swore under her breath and moved closer to them. "Put down the toy, both of you. Four stuffed dragons are more than enough for one person, wouldn't you say?"

"Estelle... be careful." I looked for backup, but Aunt Candace had unhelpfully vanished. No doubt she'd moved to a safe distance to take notes while the shifter growled under his breath. He wasn't going to shift into a wolf in public, was he?

I reached into my pocket for my wand as the growl deepened—but it was the child who shifted into a wolf rather than her dad. The cherubic little girl became a fluffy ball of claws and teeth and leaped headfirst at the stall, grabbing for the stuffed dragon.

The rat shifter yelped and dove to the side to avoid being trampled, and the sound of splintering wood filled the air as the kid barrelled straight *through* the back of the stall—right over the edge of the street towards the beach below.

Estelle flicked her wand in the nick of time, stopping the small wolf shifter's fall and then levitating her back to her father's side.

"That was a close call." Estelle lowered her wand as the young shifter's feet touched the ground. "Please—be careful."

The larger shifter glared at her. "That was your fault. Look how unsafe that is." He gestured at the splintered remains of the stall and the stuffed dragons lying in the wreckage.

"Whoa." I stepped in. "Estelle saved your kid from falling. Don't blame her."

The girl abruptly shifted back into a human and screamed at the top of her lungs. The noise drew the attention of the frizzy-haired witch from earlier, who promptly began shouting at the large shifter. At least they weren't yelling at Estelle any longer, but the guy running the stall looked at the ruined pile of wooden planks in despair. Young werewolves looked more like cuddly puppies than the deadly giant killing machines their parents became, but that didn't mean they couldn't do any damage when they threw a tantrum.

"I'm sorry," Estelle said to the rat shifter. "I'll help you fix the damage, but I might have to wait until it's quieter."

"Thanks." As the bickering pair and their wailing kid left the seafront behind, he gingerly picked up the cuddly dragon toy they'd dropped. "Those people are nothing but trouble. Who needs five of these things anyway?"

"It's a substitute for terrible parenting," said Aunt Candace, who'd materialised again with her pen and notebook in hand. Typical of her. She showed up whenever there was a crisis and then mysteriously disappeared whenever we needed her help.

"This isn't funny, Aunt Candace," said Estelle. "I feel sorry for their kid, really. Her parents aren't together any longer but they both wanted to bring her to the carnival, so they've been trying to outdo one another all day."

"I feel sorrier for anyone who has to listen to that abominable racket," said Aunt Candace as the child began wailing again. "If you or Cass had done that as kids, I'd have locked you in the basement."

"You spent all your time upstairs anyway," Estelle said.

"Were you still living in the library when Estelle and Cass were kids?" I asked curiously.

"Obviously," my aunt replied. "I let my sister and her husband deal with their tantrums."

That figured. Not that I really blamed her. Cass was difficult enough to deal with as an adult, and frankly, I didn't want to imagine her as a teenager.

"Speaking of Cass," I said, "where's she gone? Not back to the library?"

"No clue." Estelle moved to help the rat shifter pick up some of the broken planks of wood from the wreckage the rampaging shifter kid had caused.

"Thanks," he said to Estelle, picking up one of the remaining cuddly dragons. "I didn't prepare for one person to try to win my entire stock."

"I have some more in the library, don't worry," Estelle said. "I had an inkling they'd be popular, but maybe not that much."

"Good." He set about retrieving the buckets into which tourists had to throw the tennis balls in order to win a prize. "Blast. She knocked the tennis balls into the sea."

I followed his gaze. Sure enough, the yellow tennis balls had been sent flying during the shifter's rampage and were currently floating amid the waves that lapped around the pier.

"Anyone want to go for a swim?" Aunt Candace asked in a mischievous tone.

"No thanks." I gave her a stern look. "You can always make yourself useful and get them out yourself."

I pulled out my wand to retrieve them, only to take a surprised step back when the three tennis balls rose into the air before I could cast a spell. All three balls landed in the buckets at the same time, causing the rat shifter to do a double take.

"What..." He trailed off when Cass walked over, a smug smile on her face.

"You're welcome," she called to us.

"Cass?" Estelle looked startled, too, most likely for the same reasons as me—namely, the rarity of her sister doing something nice for someone. "I wondered where you'd gone."

"Thank you," the rat shifter said to Cass. "I should give you a prize for that."

"No thanks," was Cass's response, signalling an end to her brief spell of goodwill.

"You don't want a cuddly toy dragon, then?" I grinned in Cass's direction. "Might be something for you to give your pet kelpie..."

"He'd eat it," said Cass. "I don't play silly games."

"I do," said Aunt Candace. "Can I have a go?"

Honestly.

The bemused shifter handed over the tennis balls, and my aunt successfully launched one of them into the bucket and then did a celebratory dance. Cass rolled her eyes and walked away, while Aunt Candace swore when she missed the second target.

"You can have another go," offered the rat shifter.

"Don't encourage her," I said. "We should go."

Aunt Candace gave me a disgruntled look. "Spoilsport."

"There aren't many prizes left, and other people deserve a chance to win," I pointed out. "Aunt Adelaide is probably looking for us too."

Estelle nodded. "Yeah, I should keep watch to make sure that family of troublemakers doesn't come back."

"Come on." I beckoned to a reluctant Aunt Candace, who shook her head at me.

"Why the rush to leave?" she asked. "Have a date, do you?"

"No, it's raining, and we need to check the book-wyrms are definitely gone from the library—and stop Cass from smuggling any of them upstairs." I added the last part in an undertone.

"Why not?" she queried. "It'd be a laugh."

"No, it would not." Book-wyrms bred like rabbits, as we'd discovered when we'd found the mess they'd made of the History Section, and if Cass adopted a pair, they'd take over the entire third floor by the week's end. "Also, I thought you wanted me to help you with your research."

Meaning she wanted to watch me translate my dad's journal from the obscure code he'd written it in to plain English so she could swipe some ideas for her books. I figured she wouldn't be able to resist that, and sure enough, Aunt Candace grinned. "Yes, I think you need to hurry up and find me some good material, wouldn't you agree, Rory?"

"I think you need to exercise some patience." I sometimes had regrets about giving her permission to use some details of my dad's history in her novels because she insisted on hovering over my shoulder while I translated the code in which he'd written his journal entries and then got irritable when the passages turned out to concern laundry or train timetables instead of exciting adventures.

"Me? I have the patience of a saint." She sauntered off, while I followed to make sure she didn't go wandering off again.

I found Aunt Adelaide near the road that led back to the library, along with a disgruntled-looking Cass. If I had to guess, my aunt had waylaid her youngest daughter on her way back to the library.

"Ready to head back?" she asked me. "We can always pay another visit after dark when it's less crowded."

"It's never going to be less crowded," Cass griped. "You don't need to babysit me."

"I need your help with wyrm-proofing the valuable books," said Aunt Adelaide. "Only Estelle needs to supervise the carnival. The rest of you can be spared."

Estelle was head of the library's social events, so she'd taken on responsibility for the summer carnival as well as a series of events in the library itself for the local children who were at home for the summer holidays. Having an indoor option was a good move given that it had scarcely stopped raining since mid-July, but that made it even more essential that we evicted the library's unwanted guests.

Honestly, I'd have rather helped with wyrm-proofing the cabinets than deal with my aunt trying to distract me while I translated my dad's journal entries. At first, I'd been keen to translate every word to find out everything he'd wanted to keep from the Founders, but I hadn't found another mention of them since the first adventure he'd recorded, in which he'd clashed with the vampires over his search for a particular rare book. Sometimes I wondered if the Founders wanted the journal solely so nobody else would be aware of those books' existence at all, as they didn't sound that valuable or dangerous.

Aunt Candace, of course, was endlessly fascinated and didn't seem to care that the mere existence of the journal had been enough to land us on the Founders' list of enemies. Mortimer Vale had been arrested, along with his close conspirators, but that didn't mean the Founders were finished with me yet.

Nor the other vampires—especially when I owed one of them a favour. Despite her manipulative nature, Evangeline wasn't on the side of the Founders herself. She was entirely self-interested and notably interested in the journal herself, but that wasn't the same as wanting me dead. Yet a familiar tension gripped my shoulders when I saw someone waiting next to the library's doorstep and then relaxed when it became clear that it wasn't a vampire. Not even close.

Xavier, my boyfriend and the local apprentice Reaper, raised his head and smiled at me, which kicked off a flurry of warm tingles inside my chest. I smiled back as I approached him, ignoring Cass's eye roll, while my family members entered the library ahead of us.

With one exception. When I saw Aunt Candace's notebook and pen bouncing up and down in midair, I reached out a hand to swat them aside.

"What are you doing?" she protested.

"Stopping you from taking notes," I said sternly. "I told you—Xavier and I have *not* given you permission to put our relationship into your list of book ideas."

"Yet," she said, but when I gave her a warning look, she relented, entering the library behind the others.

"I don't mind her taking inspiration from us," Xavier ventured.

"I think your boss would though." Our relationship broke tradition and even skewed close to breaking the fundamental rules of the Reapers, as well, since they weren't supposed to have relationships with humans. While Xavier and I had reached a mutual understanding with his boss, that didn't mean the Grim Reaper wouldn't stand in our way again if we crossed a line.

"True." He indicated the library. "Should we go in?"

"You're not here on official Reaper business, are you?" I asked suspiciously.

"No, of course not." He tucked a strand of hair behind my ear and kissed me. "I was going to come and meet you at the pier, but I saw how crowded it was out there and figured I was better off keeping my distance."

"Wise idea." I pushed open the door and walked with him into the library. "We can go back later when it's quieter."

"To the tunnel of love?" Sylvester cackled at us from the front desk, where he'd made himself at home in our absence. The large owl's wings spread across the record book, and he swallowed the tail of what looked suspiciously like a book-wyrm.

"There isn't one," I said. "Have you been *eating* the wyrms?"

The owl belched in answer. Honestly. I wasn't sure he needed to eat at all. He might look like an owl, but he was actually a genius loci, aka the sentient embodiment of the library itself, as well as a royal pain in the neck.

"Hello, Xavier," said Aunt Adelaide from the corridor leading to our family's living quarters. "Will you be staying for dinner this time?"

"Only if everyone is on their best behaviour." I gave a pointed look at Sylvester. "Human or otherwise."

"Your wish is my command," said Sylvester. "I think I will have a nap."

Good. Sylvester and I had a complicated relationship. He liked to remind me that if not for him, the library wouldn't even exist, to which I replied that the library would have no purpose without someone to run it. Meaning my family. I figured I was justified in, say, shutting him out of my room when Xavier and I wanted some quiet time together. Those moments were generally in short supply given how hectic my life was, but I was trying to see that as a good thing. I'd lived a predictable life once before, and I never wanted to go back to that again.

"I'd be delighted to stay," Xavier answered my aunt.

Beaming, Aunt Adelaide ducked out of sight while Xavier took my hand. "Is that okay with you?"

"Sure." My brain short-circuited as he pulled me in for a kiss. "Now... what was I saying again?"

"You weren't." He smiled against my lips. "Pity there isn't a tunnel of love at the pier, really."

I grinned back. "A Reaper and a human on the tunnel of love. What a visual."

"It's not that unusual."

True. My current life might be unconventional, but it was mine. I kissed him again. "You're right. That's enough talking."

2

"Cock-a-doodle-doo!" A loud cry—which sounded more like an owl than a cockerel—hit my eardrums and woke me from sleep in an instant.

"Ow!" I sat upright then fell back onto the bed when I remembered Xavier was there—or he had been, at any rate. Now I opened my eyes properly, all that remained of him was the Reaper-shaped imprint in the mattress. "Sylvester, what are you doing?"

More to the point, what had happened to the locking spell I'd put on the door to keep out any intruders?

"Waking you up," said the owl.

"I'm aware of that," I said. "I meant *why are you in my room*? What did you do to Xavier?"

"Me?" The owl landed on the bed and dug his claws into my legs through the duvet, and I scrambled upright with a yelp of pain. "I assume he went out on Reaping Business."

"Don't joke about that, Sylvester." While it was true that Xavier might have used his Reaper disappearing trick at some point during the night and not necessarily to Reap someone's soul, I was more inclined to suspect the owl's involvement. "How did you get into my room?"

I should have seen this coming. After all, he'd kept his word and stayed out of the way when my family had got together for dinner, and the evening had been a little *too* perfect, in hindsight. Aunt Candace had kept her intrusive questions to a minimum while even Cass and Laney were almost civil to one another for the brief time they interacted —which admittedly wasn't that long since Laney lived exclusively on blood these days and didn't join us for dinner. Still. What was Sylvester up to this time?

"It's not a joke." He flapped his wings at me, creating the effect of a loud fan that made me jump out of the bed in exasperation. "I'm here because it's an emergency, you dim-witted treacle tart. You might want to go to the seafront."

"Why?" The ominous note to his words was the only thing that stopped me from shaking him off my bed and going straight back to sleep.

"Because the uglier version of your boyfriend was there earlier."

"What?" Who...? *Oh.* Right, he meant the Grim Reaper... and if the Grim Reaper had been to the pier, it could only be for one reason. "If you're telling the truth, then go and tell Aunt Adelaide, not me."

I shooed Sylvester out of my room before grabbing my clothes and shoving them on as fast as possible. Carrying my cloak over one shoulder and my bag in my hand, I ran out into the corridor, where I encountered a bleary-eyed Estelle.

"Huh? What's going on?" she asked.

"Sylvester woke me up to say the Grim Reaper's been at the pier," I explained. "I'm sorry, Estelle."

The colour drained from her face. "No."

She disappeared back into her room, while I made for the stairs. When I heard the warning noise of Aunt Candace above my head, I quickened my pace, reaching the living room mere moments before she came thundering downstairs with the speed of a charging boar.

"Wait!" I called to her. "Slow down."

"Can't talk. There's a story waiting for me out there." She ran, her dressing gown billowing behind her, while my familiar, Jet, came flitting down in her wake.

I flagged down the little crow. "Did you tell her? You didn't, did you?"

"I thought you didn't want to be disturbed, partner!" Jet squeaked.

"I didn't, but—I have no idea how Sylvester got around the locking charm on my door." I supposed that if the library thought the situation constituted an emergency, it would have let him in regardless of whatever spells I cast to seal the door shut. "Jet, did you see what happened out there?"

The front door slammed behind Aunt Candace, and then Aunt Adelaide came downstairs with Estelle on her heels.

"That owl." Aunt Adelaide tutted then spotted me in the entryway to the living room. "What did Sylvester tell you, Rory?"

"He said the Grim Reaper was at the pier, but I don't know why he decided I needed to know first," I said. "Xavier wasn't even there."

Though it explained why he'd left. Likely the Grim Reaper had been irritated at spending his night Reaping souls while Xavier was sound asleep in the library, pretending to be a regular human.

"I saw his boss, partner!" Jet squeaked. "At the pier. He's scary, isn't he?"

"Yes, he is," said Aunt Adelaide, pulling on her cloak. "Normally I'd say it's none of our business, but Candace has already left—"

"And I'm running the carnival," Estelle broke in. "If someone died there, it's on me."

"It isn't, Estelle," I insisted. "The carnival closed at midnight, didn't it?"

She compressed her lips and pulled on her own cloak before she followed her mother out of the library. Jet perched anxiously on my shoulder as I walked out into another windy, drizzly day. As the carnival had yet to open for the day, nothing remained of yesterday's crowd but empty stalls and deserted rides. An eerie silence hung over the seafront, broken only by the sound of Aunt Candace's pen scribbling in her notebook as she peered down at the gentle sloping sands of the beach.

A man lay facedown in the shallows, a wooden spike sticking out of his back.

"He's a vampire," Aunt Candace announced. "Someone staked him through the back. Straight to the heart."

Estelle sucked in a breath. "That stake... I know where it came from."

I followed her gaze to the pile of wooden planks that were all that remained of the stall the shifter child had broken during her tantrum. "Oh no."

"I should have fixed it." Estelle groaned faintly. "This is my fault."

"Don't be ridiculous," I told her. "If you had, then the person who did this would have picked up something else to use as a stake."

Not that that was much of a comfort to the guy who'd

died, but who could have possibly sneaked up on a vampire without being detected?

"Police coming through." Edwin, the elf who led the local police force, appeared behind Aunt Adelaide. Two troll bodyguards flanked him, their huge bodies crammed into uniforms and their hands big enough to crush a man's skull. "What is this?"

"Someone staked a vampire," Aunt Candace announced, her tone entirely too cheerful for the sombre occasion. "They literally stabbed him in the back. Lover's quarrel, maybe?"

Aunt Adelaide shot her a warning look before addressing Edwin with an apologetic tone. "A couple of our familiars saw him and came back to the library instead of telling you first. I'll ask them to inform the police immediately if they see anything similar in future."

"I should hope this won't be a regular occurrence," Edwin responded. "Isn't your library organising the event at the seafront?"

"I am, yes," Estelle said tremulously. "But the carnival closed at midnight. Nobody should have been here."

"This isn't her responsibility." I hadn't intended to get involved, but it was hardly fair of anyone to pin the blame on Estelle.

"I didn't imply it was," Edwin said gravely. "That said, I'd appreciate it if you let me know exactly what your familiars told you."

Did he want to hear that the Grim Reaper had been here? Probably not, though the fact that the victim had been a vampire explained why the Grim Reaper had come here himself instead of calling his apprentice. Yet he'd seemingly called Xavier back to his side regardless. That or Xavier had left of his own accord.

With good reason. As Estelle moved in to talk to Edwin, I leaned over to whisper to Aunt Adelaide, "Someone's going to have to alert you-know-who."

I didn't need to speak the name of the head vampire for her to know precisely who I meant. If Evangeline hadn't heard about the murder yet, then someone needed to enlighten her... if they didn't mind facing the backlash of her learning one of her people had been staked. In other words, we might be a little short on volunteers.

"Not you, Rory," Aunt Adelaide said firmly.

"What about your friend?" asked Cass from behind us. "Can't she break the bad news?"

I swivelled to face my cousin. "I didn't know you were awake."

"I wouldn't be if not for Aunt Candace having the subtlety of a rampaging manticore." Cass yawned. "Though your friend might want to avoid the spotlight, considering she went out last night herself."

"She did what?" My heart gave an uneasy twinge. *Laney was out last night?*

"Went out. No idea where to." Cass gave a shrug. "She didn't get back until the early hours."

"How did you know?" I'd thought Cass slept up on the third floor with her animals rather than in her own room, and she'd only increased that habit after Laney had moved into the library.

She arched a brow. "That's what concerns you? Not your friend's nocturnal wandering?"

It wasn't unusual for Laney to go wandering around at night, but if she'd seen what had happened to the vampire, she'd have told one of us. Right?

"I'll talk to her when she's awake later," I answered. "But

no, I'm not asking her to tell you-know-who that someone murdered one of her fellow vampires."

"None of us should," said Aunt Adelaide firmly. "This doesn't have anything to do with our family."

"Except for me." Estelle returned to my side, while Edwin and his troll guards went down to the beach for a closer look at the body. "I should have checked in at the carnival at closing time."

"I doubt that guy was at the carnival." I indicated the vampire's sprawling body. "There aren't a lot of vampires willing to put up with that level of noise. Besides, he might have been on the other side of town at that point."

Vampires moved with a speed no human could match and a level of stealth that made the rest of us look like bulls in china shops by comparison, which was why one of them being stabbed in the back was a rarity. If a human had killed him, even more so.

"Good point, but Evangeline might not see it that way." She spoke in a low voice as if concerned that speaking her name would draw the vampires' leader out of the shadows. Not an irrational assumption since Evangeline already had her eye on my family due to her position as Laney's teacher. Not to mention the favour I owed her.

Edwin cleared his throat. "I'm going to have to ask you all to leave."

"Of course." Aunt Adelaide made to grab her sister's arm, but Aunt Candace slithered out of the way. "Candace, come on. I'm sure Rory's familiar will give you the details later."

I looked for Jet and saw that he'd perched on a post at the end of the pier, a prime eavesdropping location. *Figures.*

"Technically he's *my* familiar." I gave Aunt Candace a pointed look. "Not your personal spy."

"Who else would give me the gossip I need?" She put on a reproachful look. "I thought we had an understanding."

"Jet can stay, but only if you come back to the library," I told her. "You don't actually want to be here when Evangeline inevitably shows up, do you?"

"Don't say her name!" she said. "Or else you'll summon her."

Cass snorted behind her. "Only when Rory says her name. The rest of us are fine."

"Don't even joke about that, Cass." Estelle gave a final worried glance down at the beach before turning away.

"Did I say I was joking?" Cass followed the others while I hovered on the spot, torn. In usual circumstances, I'd have leapt at the chance to avoid another chat with Evangeline, but avoiding her might be delaying the inevitable. After all, Laney had been out at the same time as the vampire's murder...

Don't think about that, Rory. Yes, Laney had had a brief career as a vigilante vampire hunter back when she'd first wandered into the magical world, but the vampires she'd targeted had been threatening my life. She wouldn't have staked any of the locals without telling me. I knew that.

But would Evangeline be as easily convinced?

Whatever the case, if Laney really had been out last night, I couldn't put her safety at risk by contacting Evangeline myself. Instead, I returned to the library with the others. Even Aunt Candace didn't raise a fuss at being herded back indoors. She might have a lax relationship with danger when it came to researching potential book ideas, but nobody in their right mind wanted to be near Evangeline when she discovered one of her people had been murdered.

As for Cass... well, she certainly had a reckless streak

when it came to magical monsters, but that didn't extend to the vampires. I didn't envy Edwin, but he at least had signed up to deal with situations like this when he'd become the head of the police force.

As we approached the library, my phone buzzed with a message from Xavier. *Sorry, my boss called me out early this morning. You'll probably get this message after you've already woken up and found out why, but I'd be a lot more relaxed if you stayed in the library today. Can you do that?*

I'll try, I replied.

The library had a tendency to scramble my phone signal, and it didn't help that Xavier lived in a graveyard with a guy who didn't know the meaning of the word Wi-Fi, but at least I knew where he was. I didn't have to worry about him.

Laney, though...

"Rory?" Aunt Adelaide beckoned me into the library. "Can you watch the front desk for a bit? I have to make sure the book-wyrms didn't come back overnight, and Estelle has activities to set up in the Reading Corner."

"Oh, sure." My head was not in the right place to deal with the public, but I didn't particularly want to go on book-wyrm watch, either, especially if Sylvester had been snacking on them. Cass had vanished up to the third floor as per usual while Aunt Candace was in her room, but at least they hadn't gone back to the beach.

Why was Laney out last night though? And where? There were only so many places of interest in a small town like ours, which didn't have much in the way of nightlife, unless she'd gone farther afield. Her newly acquired vampire super-speed meant she could technically walk to London and back overnight on foot without breaking a sweat, so it wasn't impossible. It was also better than some of the alternatives.

After I'd set up the front desk—and cleaned up what was left of Sylvester's midnight wyrm feast—I went to grab some coffee and toast from the kitchen. The discovery of the vampire's dead body had somewhat dampened my appetite, but I'd need the energy if Estelle had planned another day of indoor activities for the local kids. Given the rain I could hear through the front door, I had an inkling the outdoor part of the carnival wouldn't have been as popular today even if someone hadn't been murdered.

"I already planned for it to be an indoor day, but that's downright unpleasant," Estelle remarked on her way out of the kitchen with a piece of toast in hand, indicating the rain washing down the window. "Not a bad omen, I hope."

I watched the rain for a moment. "Maybe Evangeline's wrath has influenced the weather."

"Don't even." She shuddered. "She must have found out, right?"

"If not, she will. Soon."

As long as her anger didn't come back to our doorstep, we'd be able to keep out of this one, but I knew better than to make assumptions when the vampires were involved. After all, nobody ever crossed Evangeline and went unchallenged.

3

Despite the disruption, the library opened at the usual time, and Estelle shed her morose expression when the first batch of schoolchildren showed up for the day's workshop. I declined to help her teach them to write poetry, preferring to stay at the front of the library where I could keep an eye on the door.

The first part of the day passed without a hitch, but even the sound of excitable children vying for Estelle's attention and squealing over Spark the pixie wasn't enough to lure me into a false sense of security. In fact, I asked Estelle if she wouldn't mind taking the kids into a classroom instead of the Reading Corner to lessen the odds of anyone ending up traumatised when the inevitable storm arrived on our doorstep.

While I'd been mentally prepared for the moment, I still jumped when the library's door flew wide open and Evangeline strode into the lobby. Despite the gust of wind and rainwater she brought with her, not a single drop landed on her immaculate clothes or her porcelain face. Her expression, however, was wrathful enough to make a thunderstorm seem like a mild breeze in comparison.

"Evangeline." By habit, I focused my attention on the desk and not on her face so as not to give away my private thoughts. "Can I help you?"

"Yes," she said, her voice vibrating with anger. "You can help me by waking that friend of yours."

My mouth parted. "Laney? Why?"

"Don't play the fool, Aurora. It's unbecoming of you."

My heartbeat thrummed in my chest, and my hand inched towards my pocket, where I'd stashed my Biblio-Witch Inventory. I'd been learning ways to defend myself from the vampires in case of future incidents with the Founders, but Evangeline could rip out my jugular with a flick of her fingers, and even the magic at my fingertips wouldn't spare my life.

"I am not looking for a fight," she said as if she'd sensed my thoughts—which was distinctly possible. "Unless your friend has a reason to hide."

"She's not hiding, she's asleep," I countered. "And—look, this is about the guy who was staked at the beach, right? Laney had nothing to do with that."

"You haven't spoken to her since last night, have you?" she queried. "I'm guessing not, and you cannot deny that she has been known to use that particular method of dispatching her targets."

"When she killed those other vampires, she did it to protect me." I swallowed, my throat dry. "Was the man who died from Ivory Beach?"

"Yes, he was one of my own." Her pointed teeth bared in a snarl. "There will be blood for this."

Oh boy. "I'm sorry, but I can guarantee Laney didn't kill

him. She knows what she'd risk by turning against any of your people."

"Does she now?" She moved imperceptibly, raising her head as if reacting to something I couldn't hear myself, which intensified the impression of a predator ready to pounce. "I'm not convinced, Aurora. Your friend is as reckless as she was as a human, maybe more so, and she takes great pains to try to hide her thoughts from me."

My heart lurched. Most of Laney's desire to hide her thoughts came out of the impulse to prevent Evangeline from finding out the contents of my dad's journal. I hadn't known it had actually been effective, much less that Evangeline would have noticed.

"The other vampires she killed were linked to the Founders," I said carefully. "There aren't any here, so she wouldn't have reason to..." I faltered as she moved forwards again, her attention focusing on a spot somewhere behind me.

"Come out," she said. "I know you're listening to us."

Aunt Adelaide walked into view, her Biblio-Witch Inventory in one hand and her face free of its usual cheer. "What are you doing here, Evangeline?"

"I'm here to talk to a guest of yours," she said. "If she comes downstairs of her own accord, then I'll have no need to disturb the rest of you."

"If you're talking about who I think you are, she's not a guest," my aunt replied. "She's a resident of the library."

My heartbeat quickened at the visible annoyance in Evangeline's expression. Denying her request wouldn't be wise, but I could only imagine the chaos if Evangeline unleashed the extent of her anger upon the library. Really, I was glad I'd asked Estelle to move her poetry workshop out of the line of fire. We didn't need to deal with a bunch of complaints from angry parents on top of the wrath of the head vampire.

"Regardless," Evangeline said, "I'd advise you to wake her and tell her to come to my home to speak with me in person. If she fails to show up within the hour, then I'll come back myself, and I won't be so patient with you next time."

She vanished in a blink, the door flitting shut behind her and a chill lingering in her wake.

I released a shaky breath. "Aunt Adelaide, did you guess she was going to come here?"

"I hoped I was wrong." She pocketed her Biblio-Witch Inventory. "You can wake Laney yourself, Rory, if you prefer."

"Laney can't have killed that guy." Even if he *had* been linked to the Founders, she'd have told one of us first, though Evangeline would not appreciate the insinuation that the enemy had been hiding among her people. Besides, Laney knew better than to use the vigilante justice approach now she was one of the vampires herself. Didn't she?

When my aunt didn't reply, I frowned. "You don't think she did, do you? Is that why you expected Evangeline?"

"No, but I thought Evangeline might come to call in her favour," said Aunt Adelaide.

"She still might." It was Laney I was more worried for. Laney was no pushover these days, but defying Evangeline meant facing death in the permanent sense. "Let's get this over with."

I crossed the lobby, climbed the stairs leading up to our rooms, and knocked on Laney's door. When she didn't answer, I knocked again, louder.

After the third knock, Laney emerged, blearily looking at me. Even half asleep, she had the languid grace of a vampire, her skin free of blemishes and her hair silky smooth instead of sticking up like mine would have been if I'd been dragged out of bed. "What... Rory?"

"Sorry," I said to her. "I have bad news. A vampire showed up staked to death last night. Evangeline wants to talk to you."

Laney went from sleepy to alert in a second, jumping back a step with the swiftness of a startled cat. "No way. She knows I wouldn't have killed one of her people. Doesn't she?"

"I know you didn't do it," I said to her. "I don't know that she's going to take no for an answer, though, and she asked you to come to her home to talk to her in person."

Laney tugged a hand through her glossy dark hair. "Right... I'll come downstairs in a second."

"I can go with you," I offered.

"No way. Not if she's looking for a punching bag." She vanished back into her room. "I'll be right down."

Before I reached the foot of the stairs, she was back, and she'd changed into a fresh outfit. Vampire super-speed saved an awful lot of time, that was for sure.

"I won't let you go alone," I told her. "No way."

"I'm tougher than I look, remember?"

I knew that, but Evangeline was right when she said my best friend had a reckless streak that had intensified when she'd become immortal. That didn't mean she'd cross the line and murder her fellow vampires, and Evangeline would only need to take a small look into her thoughts to know that.

"Rory, I'll be fine," she insisted. "I have no idea who was murdered, and she'll see the truth for herself the instant she looks into my head."

"I didn't know you were having that much success keeping her out." Vampires generally found it easy to shield their thoughts against their fellow mind readers, but someone as powerful as Evangeline would be able to stride past the defences of all but the strongest vampires. Since she was overseeing Laney's vampire training personally, they spent a lot of time together, which made slipups even more likely to occur.

"I've been working on it." She glided alongside me into the lobby, as elegant as ever despite having woken up from a dead sleep not a minute beforehand. "I won't let her get a single glimpse of the journal."

My throat closed up. "That's not the issue here."

Yes, I'd gone to every length to keep Evangeline from learning the contents of my dad's private journal, but I knew the risks I'd taken when I'd brought Laney into my confidence. Keeping my secrets wasn't worth her life.

"I'll be fine." She made for the front door, briefly halting to give my aunt an encouraging nod.

"I hope you're right," said Aunt Adelaide.

Laney shot me a smile and disappeared through the front door. I dragged my gaze away and spotted movement out of the corner of my eye up on the stairs leading to the upper balconies. I raised my head, and Cass, who'd evidently been watching the whole time, saw me looking at her and vanished amid the shelves. *Oh boy.*

"How long should I leave it before I go after her?" I asked Aunt Adelaide. "Half an hour? More?"

"Rory," said Aunt Adelaide in a gentle tone. "Don't worry. She'll come back."

"I know." I heaved a sigh. "It strikes me as a bad sign that she's the first person Evangeline thought of when someone got staked to death though."

"Not necessarily," said Aunt Adelaide. "Laney is the newest vampire, isn't she?"

"I thought so, but isn't it more likely to have been a non-vampire who killed him?" Sneaking up on one of them wasn't easy, but staking a fellow vampire to death didn't sound characteristic of one of the undead. "I've never seen that guy before, so I've no idea who he is."

"Then go and find out," said Aunt Candace, poking her head out of an alcove. "Go to the vampires' home and ask some questions."

"No," said Aunt Adelaide. "Absolutely not, Candace. You're not thinking of going yourself?"

Aunt Candace rarely came out of her writing cave during the day, but I should have guessed she'd heard our conversation with Evangeline. She wouldn't have wanted to miss a minute of the drama.

"I don't currently have any plans to, no," said Aunt Candace.

"Good," said Aunt Adelaide. "Don't make any. I don't need to worry about you as well as Rory and Laney."

My heart dropped. "You don't have to worry about me *or* Laney. I can do enough worrying for the pair of us."

She gave me a kind smile. "I think you know that isn't how it works, Rory."

A lump rose in my throat. "I brought Laney into this myself, remember? I'm not much of a friend if I leave her to deal with this alone."

"Laney herself wouldn't want you to put yourself at risk," Aunt Adelaide said. "If it were anyone else threatening her, I might say differently... but you can't challenge Evangeline."

I knew that, but I'd also crossed more lines with Evangeline than the average person and still managed to keep my head. I owed her a favour, and my entanglement with the Reapers wasn't easily forgotten either.

"Pity we regular people can't learn how to mind-read," Aunt Candace said in a thoughtful tone.

"You spend enough time collecting gossip from my familiar," I pointed out. "We don't need you poking into everyone's thoughts as well."

"A shame if you ask me." She retreated into the living quarters with a cackle, while I resolved to stay within sight of the door in case she got it into her head to slip out of the library after all.

"I'll keep an eye on her," said Aunt Adelaide. "Rory, can you help with those returns? They've piled up while I was checking on the book-wyrm situation."

"Sure," I said. "The wyrms haven't come back, then?"

"No, and I'll keep my fingers crossed that they'll stay that way," she replied.

"Unless we can weaponise them against Evangeline." Xavier would want to know, so I sent him a message explaining the situation and then busied myself returning books to the correct shelves in order to take my mind off Laney.

Half an hour passed before the front door fluttered inwards, and I dropped the book I'd been holding. The book yowled at me like an angry cat, but I was so relieved to see Laney that I hardly noticed.

"Laney." I strode to her, seeing that she was slightly damp but otherwise intact "Are you okay?"

Laney sucked in a breath she didn't need to take, an old habit that betrayed her relief. "Yeah. I *think* she believed me when I said I had nothing to do with that guy's death, but it was hard to let her into my thoughts. I've got into the habit of doing the opposite."

"I wouldn't have minded if she'd seen a few pages of the journal," I told her. "It's hardly incriminating, believe me."

I hadn't found anything that might have reason to interest the Founders recently, anyway.

"It's your business, not hers," Laney said. "It's fine. I got out alive."

"You did." Yet a sense of wariness lingered in her manner. "She doesn't know who killed that guy, then?"

"No, she doesn't," she said. "Which is why it's perplexing that she won't let Edwin get a look-in. She told me that since the victim was a vampire, she'll look into the guy's murder herself, without the police's input."

I winced. "I bet Edwin isn't thrilled."

"Nope," she said. "Especially as he found Jeffrey's body first—that's the guy's name, which is kinda bland for a vampire, if you ask me."

Poor Edwin. What could he do though? He might be the head of the police, but he had no magical skills of his own, and the only person in town who might be a match for the head vampire was the notoriously impartial Grim Reaper. Edwin would have to cave in, if just to save his own neck. Literally.

Laney yawned. "I'm going back to bed. Wake me up if she comes back."

"She'd better not."

As she returned to the living quarters, I caught Aunt Adelaide's eye. She smiled when she saw me looking at her. "That's that taken care of."

"For now."

If even Evangeline didn't have any idea who the killer was, then this wasn't over. Not by a long shot.

DESPITE MY LINGERING JUMPINESS, I offered to take over the front desk again once I'd finished dealing with the returns. As a result, I was alone at the front of the lobby when we had our second unwelcome visitor of the day.

Shortly before my lunch break, the front door opened, and Edwin shuffled into the library. For once, he was without the troll guards who usually flanked him, and he looked decidedly harried.

"Hey, Edwin," I said to the elf policeman. "Something wrong?"

"You might say that," he said. "As you should know given that you saw it for yourself."

"You mean the murder?" Suspicion rose. "Evangeline decided to take over your murder investigation, didn't she? You didn't tell her otherwise?"

"No, I most certainly did not," he said. "How did you know? Your friend?"

"Evangeline questioned her," I explained. "I get the impression the head vampire isn't acting entirely rationally. Would I be correct?"

"She refuses to work with me." Two spots of colour appeared high on his cheeks. "Refuses to *respect* me, in fact, or let me do my job."

"Thought so." I didn't envy his position. "Why are you here, then?"

"Because you've worked with her before."

"Oh no." I held up my hands. "I thought you told me *not* to get involved in police investigations."

"That was directed more at certain family members of yours." He paced in front of the desk, wringing his hands. "I have every intention of investigating this murder myself, but to do that, I need the cooperation of the vampires' leader.

You have a working relationship with Evangeline, Rory. You can't deny it."

"I owe her a favour," I said. "Not the other way around. She's already livid, and I don't need to paint another target on my head *and* Laney's by trying to convince her to work with you."

"That's not what I'm asking," he said. "I want you to negotiate with her on my behalf and bring any information she unearths on the murder directly to me."

"No." I shook my head. "That's not going to work."

"I should clarify that I'm not asking you to work for free, Aurora," he said. "We can arrange a payment if necessary."

"It's not the money, it's the threat to my life that bothers me," I told him. "Oh, and my entire family. Not to mention Laney."

"You surely do not believe that Evangeline would do you harm?" he queried. "She knows that in order to be allowed to live here in Ivory Beach, she has to abide by certain rules."

"I notice you aren't falling over yourself to pay her a home visit," I said caustically. "Edwin, I get that you're in a bind, but she has every reason *not* to trust me with important information about whoever might have murdered one of her people. If anything, I'm more closely allied with the Grim Reaper than with her."

"She's already proven that she's willing to overlook that connection if she needs your help, and I'd wager she does."

"She'd sooner stake herself in the back than admit she needs *anyone's* help, least of all a human's." What in the world was he thinking? I might be the *last* human she'd trust with important information.

"I'm not going to pressure you into making the decision right away," he said. "However, I'd prefer for this murder case to be resolved, and I think Evangeline would too. You said she questioned your friend? Did she suspect her?"

"Yes, but like I said, she's being irrational." I wished I hadn't mentioned Laney at all. She didn't need to deal with suspicion from the police as well. "She didn't even mention the favour I owe her."

"You said yourself that she'd be reluctant to admit to needing your help," he said. "I'm going to do my best to proceed alone, but the reality is that I'm only working with half the evidence."

"If another vampire is the killer, then it's her business, right?"

"And if not?" he asked. "If I back out of the case, then it'll send a message to everyone else in Ivory Beach that I'm too afraid of Evangeline to do my job."

If I was feeling vindictive, I might have mentioned that he'd proven exactly that by coming to me, but that was unfair. I'd said no myself, after all.

"I understand that," I said delicately, "but putting the burden on my family isn't something I can agree to without consulting them."

"I don't expect you to," he said. "The choice is yours. I'll leave you be."

He walked out of the door, which the wind blew closed behind him. He must be truly desperate to willingly bring me into an official investigation, and while part of me was annoyed that I was the first person he'd thought of, I *did* owe Evangeline a favour. That much couldn't be disputed.

If I offered to help her find the culprit, the worst she could do was say no, right? Laney might be off the hook for now, but I couldn't deny that she'd defied Evangeline by keeping her thoughts hidden from her, and I'd be helpless to protect her if I remained on the outskirts of the investigation.

Also, let's face it, there were far worse ways to repay my favour, and I'd have Laney's safety in my own hands. A hell of a responsibility, but better than leaving it with Evangeline.

Before I made my choice, however, I'd have to see if my family members agreed.

4

"No." Aunt Adelaide walked into view before I'd even had time to move away from the desk. "Rory, I know what you're thinking, but I can't encourage you to take the risk. You know why."

"Yeah... I do." I glanced in the direction of the Reading Corner, hoping that Estelle and her audience of schoolchildren had remained oblivious to the tense situation elsewhere in the library. "I feel like staying on the sidelines is just as much of a risk, though, at least for Laney."

"That doesn't mean you need to deliver yourself into Evangeline's hands."

"I owe her," I reminded my aunt. "If I take the chance to fulfil my end of the bargain, I'll ensure she doesn't rope me into doing any other heinous thing for her in the future. I'm essentially killing two birds with one stone."

"I don't like the sound of that one bit." Sylvester flew onto the desk, his clawed feet knocking the record book askew. "Not a bit."

You aren't even a bird, I wanted to say, but held my tongue when Jet flew down to join him.

"It's a figure of speech." I rescued the record book before the owl's flapping wings knocked it off the desk. "What do you think about it, then?"

"Concerning the vampires?" he said. "They have an admirable sense of style, I suppose, but not many other points in their favour."

"That wasn't what I... never mind." Sylvester had no doubt been listening to every word of my conversations with Edwin, Laney, *and* Evangeline, so he knew perfectly well what was going on. "Jet, do you think I should offer to help Evangeline find out who killed one of her people so I can pass on the information to Edwin?"

"It's up to you, partner!" he answered.

"I doubt Evangeline would allow you to double-cross her, Rory," said Aunt Adelaide.

"It's not double-crossing if we all have the same goal," I said. "If she won't work with Edwin directly, what are the other options? I wouldn't have to do any actual investigating, besides. I'd be a messenger bird."

"I can do that, partner!" Jet squeaked. "I'll come with you."

Aunt Adelaide sighed. "If you want to speak to her, you certainly shouldn't go alone."

"If you're sure, Jet," I said to my familiar. "I need to check with the others too. Estelle... I'll wait until she's done teaching her poetry lesson. Aunt Candace pretty much already gave me permission to go to the vampires' home. As for Cass..."

"I'll tell her," Aunt Adelaide said. "I think that'll be easier for everyone."

"She saw Laney come back," I said. "She's probably already worked it out."

Cass would be livid at my decision to involve myself in

the vampires' business again, but she was no doubt already stewing over the fact that Laney had been called in for questioning. Nothing short of my best friend leaving the library altogether would satisfy her, so worrying about what she thought of my choice was a nonstarter.

"True," said Aunt Adelaide. "I have to say, I feel as if I should make a stronger case for you staying out of this, but you're adult enough to make up your own mind."

"Edwin told me that Evangeline won't break the laws."

"Yes, and you said yourself that he wouldn't volunteer to go in your place."

"Maybe not. I won't let Laney end up being blamed for this. Not if there's anything I can do to help find the real killer."

"I won't stop you, Rory," Aunt Adelaide said. "Are you going to tell Xavier though? And his boss?"

Oh boy. There was no telling how the Grim Reaper would react given that he and Evangeline were fundamentally opposed. On the other hand, he knew full well that I owed her a favour and that I'd be powerless to resist if she called on me.

"I'll tell him," I said. "But really, this might come to nothing if she says no. I'll ask if she's open to the possibility, that's all."

Instead of hearing me out, she might shut the door in my face. In fact, part of me was sure she would. Anything rather than accepting my help, or admitting she even needed it.

As for how the Grim Reaper would respond... that would have to wait until later.

∽

I WAITED until the library closed for the day before leaving for the vampires' headquarters with Jet perched on my shoulder. Aunt Candace waved me off with a cheery "don't die" but otherwise didn't offer to come with me.

"I officially have less sense than Aunt Candace does," I remarked to Estelle.

"Rory, it's really not a good idea to put yourself in harm's way," she said. "At least when Evangeline came here, she was on our turf, not her own."

"True, but I'd prefer for her not to pay another visit to the library," I said. "If this works, I'll get myself out of debt with her *and* keep everyone safe."

"I know." She gave me a brief hug. "Please don't stay out long. If you're not back in half an hour…"

"I'll send Jet to tell you if I need anything."

My familiar was nowhere near his usual chattery self as we climbed the sloping hill of the high street to the church where the vampires made their home. The oak doors were sealed shut while the stained-glass windows were covered with enough dust to prevent any natural light from getting inside. Its spired roofs made a formidable impression against the darkening sky, and my doubts intensified. Heart in my throat, I knocked on the door.

Evangeline answered a heartbeat later, and her eyes narrowed in annoyance when she saw me outside the door. "Aurora. If your friend has more information to share, is she incapable of coming here herself?"

"I'm not here for her. I wanted to offer to help." I drew in a quick breath. "I know I owe you a favour, and that you're keen to solve this case quickly. If you need the library's resources, then I can offer those to you as well."

She stared at me for a moment. Then she laughed, a humourless sound that frankly spooked me more than any of her deadly silences. With difficulty, I resisted the impulse to back away and flee down the high street.

"You wanted to offer me a *favour*," she said. "As if you think I need one. No, this has Edwin's fingerprints all over it, and I won't have you spying on me for him."

"I'm not spying on you." I cursed the tremor in my voice. "And that's not what Edwin wants."

"No, he wants to undermine me."

"Edwin *is* the chief of police." The words stuck in my throat. "I'm not saying you aren't... aren't justified in being angry that one of your people is dead, but taking over his role puts him in a tricky position."

"That sounds like it ought to be his problem, not mine." She glowered. "I look after my own. He knows that."

"Okay." I took a step back. "I respect that, but if you don't know for sure that another vampire was the murderer, then shouldn't the police be involved in the investigation?"

"If Edwin wants to talk to me himself, then he's welcome to, but I will *not* be mocked, Aurora."

"Not my intention." Another step back. "Never mind. I'll go."

She beckoned with a finger. "Now you're here, I want a word. Without your familiar."

Jet squeaked, took flight, and landed on a nearby fence post, but I stood my ground. "Why? What do you want to talk about?"

"Aurora, I hardly think you're in a position to make demands."

"If I'm going to walk into a vampire's home, I'd like to know why." My heart beat so fast that it made me feel light-headed, and I dug my nails into my palms to keep from dissolving into pure terror. "Is it Laney? Or the Reaper?" Or my dad's journal? All three were equally likely—and also equally likely to land me in trouble. Yes, Evangeline was bound to obey the laws like everyone else in the community, but the animal instinct within me remained conscious that I was in the company of a predator. Add in her current mood and the fact that she'd kicked Edwin out of his own investigation, and I was even more reluctant to walk into a church full of furious vampires.

"Would it help if I vowed to keep you under my protection when you're in my home?" she enquired. "Nobody will harm you."

I hesitated. Maybe I *was* overthinking the matter. I'd come here intentionally, after all, and perhaps I ought to have expected her to want to discuss the murder somewhere more private. "I'd still like to know what to expect."

"You know what to expect," she said. "You've been here before."

I had. I'd attended one of her parties, in fact, and it was a miracle I'd got out of that one alive. Considering the night had ended in a vampire showing up dead, it wasn't exactly a fond memory to anyone except perhaps for Aunt Candace, but I banished the thought from my mind and turned to Jet. "I'll be okay. Wait for me, and if I don't come out soon…"

"That isn't necessary." Evangeline beckoned again with a crooked finger. "I won't keep you for long."

It wasn't much of a reassurance when a short time spent with a vampire could turn into a literal eternity. I'd made my choice, though, so I followed her through the oak doors and into the chill of her home.

Without the crowds that had thronged her gathering, the church's majesty was more obvious. The light of the setting sun spilled across the flagstones, towering pillars supported the high ceiling, and bats nested in the rafters. The church was hundreds of years old and might not even have been renovated for modern humans, considering vampires didn't need heating or plumbing or anything. I jumped when the door boomed shut behind me, unable to suppress a shiver of dread.

What was I thinking? Evangeline had somehow turned my offer of help into a trap that I'd nevertheless willingly walked straight into. It was too late for me to turn back, though, so I followed her across the flagstones to another wooden door.

Evangeline pushed the door inward, beckoning me into a small room. "This is my office."

It looked more like a prison cell, with narrow stone walls and a windowless door. Not a speck of natural light penetrated the gloom, though a flickering lamp became visible on the desk when she closed the door. So, the vampires did have electricity after all.

She caught me looking at the lamp. "We're not *that* steeped in the past, Aurora. My fellow vampires and I are willing to acknowledge that some of our contemporaries had the occasional innovative idea."

Hmm. "Right. So... what did you want to ask me?"

"I never said I wanted to ask you anything, Aurora," she said. "I simply wanted to talk in confidence, away from eavesdroppers."

What was that supposed to mean? Did she think Jet would report every word to my family, or was she more concerned that her fellow vampires would seize on the chance to listen in?

"The latter, mostly," she said.

Ack. I'd been doing my best to hide my thoughts, but the fear when I'd entered the church had scrambled my resolve. I swiftly turned my attention to the stone wall before she glimpsed any other unwanted images in my head.

"There's no need for that, Aurora," she said. "I simply wanted to learn your fears in order to assuage them."

I had my doubts that was the only reason, but I didn't intend to let her peer into my mind again if I could help it. "You know my fears. I'd like to stay alive... and mortal."

"Are you sure about that?" Her pointed teeth showed when she smiled. "I think that shedding the mask of mortality would resolve several of the dilemmas plaguing your mind. Such as the question of your friend's fate and your relationship with the immortal Reaper. Though with the latter, becoming one of us would create a new set of problems, of course."

I was barely aware of the instinctive recoil that gripped my body until my back hit the door. "Oh no. I thought you didn't call me in here to turn me into a vampire."

"I did not," she said. "I was simply responding to your comment. As to why I called you in here, you saw the body for yourself."

So, this was about the murder after all.

"I did," I said. "Someone... someone staked him to death."

"In the back." She spoke dispassionately despite the hint of anger in her eyes.

"I don't know if that means the attack was premeditated or not," I said quickly, thinking of Estelle's horror at the murderer's choice of weapon. "It seems to me that the killer just grabbed the nearest available piece of wood."

"It does," she agreed. "But that doesn't mean that everything is as it seems on the outside, don't you agree?"

"I guess." I couldn't figure out what she was trying to imply. "You think there was more to the murder? Do... do you think it was another vampire? Or an outsider?"

Anger flared in her eyes. "Both are unacceptable."

"I—know." My voice threatened to shake again. "It's either someone from the inside of the town or the outside, right?"

"A rather simplistic way of putting it."

It would help if I had an insight into *her* thoughts. "You don't think it was a non-vampire, then? I know it's hard to sneak up on one of you..."

"Usually, yes," she said. "However, the victim was newly turned. He joined us barely a month ago."

He had? I hadn't known there were any vampires newer than Laney. "You think that might be why he was targeted?"

I wished she'd give me a clue to steer me in the right direction.

"Unlikely," she said. "It does make it highly unlikely that one of my own people was responsible, though, given that he had little time to make enemies."

"But... what about his old life?" I asked. "Before he was turned?"

"I haven't the faintest interest in my recruits' former lives," she said. "I strongly encourage any vampire who joins me to leave everything behind them when their mortal existence is over, and he was no exception."

I already knew that due to her ongoing annoyance at Laney for continuing to live in the library instead of moving to the vampires' part of town. "He might still have stayed in touch with some of them. It might be worth asking Edwin..."

Her scowl made me drop that sentence before I finished. "That would be a line of questioning more suited to the police than to me."

"I thought you didn't want Edwin getting involved." If he had information on the victim's former life that Evangeline didn't, though, she'd want to know. "If I did ask him, what then?"

"I can trust you to bring any relevant information to me, can I not, Aurora?"

I gaped at her for a moment. She wanted me to do the same as Edwin had asked of me, albeit in reverse. Unless there was a trick embedded in her words.

"Just a yes or no will do, Aurora."

"Yes," I said. "I mean, I assume you don't plan to scare the living daylights out of him for doing his job."

"Not if he stays on his own side of this and not mine."

In other words, if he stuck to questioning humans, not vampires. "I'm sure he will."

"Good. You may leave."

That was it? Baffled, I tentatively opened the door, but she didn't budge, and she didn't even follow me out of the room. I crossed the flagstones on shaky legs and reached the door without being challenged or seeing another soul.

Only then did it hit me that she'd agreed to my offer without actually saying so. *Vampires.* For all her dramatics, she'd done exactly as I'd wanted. Or rather, as Edwin had wanted. Who would have thought it?

When the door closed behind me, Jet flew around my head, chirping happily. "Partner, I'm glad you're okay."

"Me too," I said. "Except I think I just made a deal with the devil."

5

When I re-entered the library, my family descended on me at the door—well, except for Cass, but I hadn't expected her to be overly concerned for my fate when I'd willingly walked into Evangeline's home.

"Rory." Aunt Adelaide peered at my face in concern. "Are you all right?"

"I'm fine." I watched Jet fly from my shoulder to Aunt Candace's, who waited with her notebook and pen bouncing up and down in the air. "Honestly, it's not that exciting an update."

"She didn't say yes?" said Estelle. "Did she?"

"Not directly, but I think that was deliberate," I explained. "She implied that Edwin and I were free to question any non-vampire, as long as I told her everything afterwards."

"Isn't that what Edwin himself asked you to do but in reverse?" Aunt Adelaide asked. "That sounds like a dangerous game to play."

"Or it might just be her being too stubborn to admit she

needs help," I said. "According to Evangeline, the vampire was newly turned. She has zero knowledge or interest in who he was when he was alive, so if the killer came from his former life, she wouldn't know."

"That's why she needs you and Edwin, then," Estelle surmised. "Interesting. Or terrifying, depending on your outlook."

"I think Rory's right and that she didn't want to admit to a lack of knowledge," said Aunt Adelaide. "That said, there's no guarantee Edwin will be able to make it far with only half the available information."

"Are you going to tell him now, then?" asked Estelle. "Or wait until tomorrow?"

"I don't want to drag this out, so I'll go now," I said. "The quicker we resolve this, the better. I know there's the poetry night this evening…"

Estelle shook her head. "I feel like surviving an encounter with Evangeline—twice—ought to count as an excuse for you to skip out on listening to the local students read out their terrible poems."

"I should tell them you said that." Aunt Candace snickered.

"Don't you want to do a reading?" I asked. "I'm sure it'll be a hit."

She gave a shudder. "I'd sooner spend the night in Evangeline's crypt."

"Don't you even think about it," Aunt Adelaide said. "You're going now, Rory? Want one of us to come with you?"

"I'll be fine," I said. "I don't want this to end up being more trouble than it's worth for you."

"I hope you're getting paid," said Aunt Candace.

"Yes, according to Edwin," I replied, "but I'm not interested in compensation. I'm more interested in keeping the vampires out of everyone's hair, including Laney's."

"So, you're playing nice with the vampires in the short-term in the hopes of a quick resolution," said Aunt Candace. "Good choice. I'd have done the same."

"Thanks?" Her comment made my choice seem even more unwise than it already did, but it couldn't be helped.

"You're welcome," she said. "Want me to wake up your vampire friend?"

"I'll tell her myself," I said. "Later. She's been through enough today already."

Come to think of it, Evangeline hadn't even mentioned Laney's name during our conversation about the murder. I hoped that meant Laney was off the suspect list for the time being, but I wouldn't mention her name in front of Edwin regardless.

As I left the library, I checked my phone for messages but found no response from Xavier. Presumably, he had yet to receive my last message, which suggested I ought to stop at the cemetery on the way to the beach. I hadn't a clue how to explain my agreement with Evangeline, let alone in front of his boss, but I'd have to face the aftermath sooner or later.

I crossed the square and walked to the cemetery, which contained the house in which Xavier and his boss lived. I pushed open the creaky gate and had barely taken two steps into the grounds before Xavier himself appeared, his expression taut with concern.

"Rory?" He drew me into a hug. "Are you okay?"

"Xavier," I breathed against his chest. "Ah... I guess you got my messages."

"I didn't." He slid his hand into mine, and despite the chill, I found my pulse relaxing at his touch. "I'm sorry I took off this morning. I sensed my boss near the beach, and when I realised that he'd Reaped the soul of a vampire, I knew he'd probably want me to come back here."

"I figured it was something like that," I said. "Jet and Sylvester were outside and saw the Grim Reaper too. That's how we ended up at the beach before the police did."

"Yes, I imagine Evangeline isn't in the best of moods," he said. "Or doesn't she know yet?"

"Er." All my rehearsed explanations flew straight out of my mind. "Yeah. She knows."

He studied my face. "Rory... what did she do?"

"It's more what *I* did." I squeezed his hand. "I'll tell you on the way to talk to Edwin."

"To *Edwin*?" he echoed. "What *did* you do, Rory?"

As we walked to the seafront, I told him everything from the moment of Evangeline's visit to the library to my own trip to her home. His expression briefly shifted from concern to anger when I brought up Edwin's request, but I made it clear that the decision to talk to Evangeline had been mine alone.

"Please don't tell me to say no to her," I added to him. "It's too late now, regardless of what your boss says. In fact, it might be best not to tell him."

"I can guarantee he'll find out one way or another," he said. "It's impossible for you to work with his mortal enemy without him taking notice."

"I'm not working with Evangeline," I said. "I'm more of a glorified messenger bird between her and Edwin because she's too stubborn to work with him directly."

"You still need to involve yourself directly in the police investigation into this vampire's death," he said. "Rory..."

"Please don't." I peered into his aquamarine eyes. "Xavier, you have to trust me on this, okay? If I see this through, everyone gets what they want. Evangeline can find her killer and enact justice if it turns out to be a vampire, and Edwin gets to keep his dignity intact."

"And his neck, I expect."

"That too." As we turned into the street that ran across the seafront, I saw the man himself pacing around his office through the front window of the police station. "This might end up being an easy crime to solve. The guy was a new vampire who probably thought he was more invincible than he actually was."

"That simple?" He tilted his head. "You don't actually believe it, Rory."

"No, but that promise I made to Evangeline has been hanging over my head for ages, and I can think of a dozen things she might ask for that are much worse than this."

"This was exactly the sort of thing I was afraid she *would* ask of you," he said. "What if the death turns out to be the Founders' work and your involvement puts you in their sights again?"

"I don't think so, somehow," I said. "Even if it is, I can't just disconnect myself from the vampires, and not just because I have one living in the library. It's never been that easy."

"I know." He exhaled in a sigh. "I'm not going to talk you out of anything, but I also can't let you do this alone."

"My entire family is trying to get in on this too. I'm far from alone, trust me."

"Yes, but I think you'd rather have me shadowing you than my boss."

"True." The Grim Reaper was as unpredictable as Evangeline, even if he wasn't as overt with his temper tantrums. "Unless... you aren't suggesting he'll find a reason to use my agreement with Evangeline against both of us?"

"I hope not," he said. "No, I doubt he would. He already knew you owed her a favour."

"Yeah, and *I* doubt Evangeline has any plans to go fishing for the Reapers' secrets when she's working with me. All she wants is to find the killer." There was the comment she'd made on my mortality, but I had no intention of mentioning that to Xavier, and it had likely been more an attempt to get under my skin than anything else. "Anyway, I need to tell Edwin why I'm lurking outside."

The doors slid open, and we both entered the police station. Edwin stood behind the wooden desk that dominated the small office, one of his troll officers lurking in the background.

"Aurora," Edwin said. "I hope you're here with positive news?"

"Yes," I said. "I spoke to Evangeline, and she agreed... well, sort of."

"She did?" Shock flitted across his expression. "That's great news."

"You didn't think she would?" Had he asked me to risk my neck for a cause he didn't believe in?

"No... I *hoped* she'd see reason," he clarified. "But one can never be certain with someone as ancient and clever as Evangeline."

"The catch is that she wants me to share everything with her," I said. "Which is the same as you asked of me."

"What?" His mouth turned down at the corners. "You're talking about sharing the details of a murder investigation with a member of the public."

My brows rose. "Does Evangeline count as a regular member of the public?"

"In this case, yes."

"You know that leaving her out of this isn't an option

even if the culprit doesn't turn out to be a vampire," I pointed out. "She knows her own people better than you do. Besides, she can read my thoughts. I thought you'd already accounted for that."

"She turned my own offer against me." His jaw clenched. "I don't appreciate being undermined."

"She's not undermining you," I said. "She said that you're entitled to do all the investigating you like, but if the killer is among her own people, it's her responsibility to deal with them. And you know, I'm not sure that's true."

He frowned. "You think it was a human who inflicted that injury on a vampire?"

"He was a new vampire, so it's more likely he made enemies *before* being a vampire than after," I explained. "Also, he was staked in the back. I don't see another vampire demonstrating that level of disrespect to one of their own."

"That's an assumption, Rory," he said. "It's not proof."

"I know, but that's why I need your input." I hadn't expected to need to be prepared to negotiate with him as much as I had with Evangeline. "Do you have a list of potential suspects he knew when he was alive? Evangeline said that she doesn't have any information on his old life. She's not interested."

"He was no longer in contact with any members of his family," he said. "From what I've seen so far, it seems as if he's lived in that ghastly church with nobody but the vampires for company for the past couple of months."

"She was hardcore when she made him cut off all contact, then," I said. "Maybe someone he used to be friends with got mad at him for ditching them."

"Again, that's speculation," he said. "I'll have a look into any possible contacts, and I'll let you know when I have an update."

"All right."

That would have to do. Come to think of it, Evangeline and I had never discussed how often she expected me to update her. It would put off our patrons to have her flitting in and out of the library on a regular basis, to say the least.

"I'll have more to tell you by tomorrow, Rory." He waved me off. "Go on."

"See you then." I left the police station, Xavier shadowing me. "I expected him to ask why you were here. You didn't use your Reaper invisibility trick, did you?"

"I thought it would be easier if I did."

"That means he thought I was talking to myself when we were outside?" I shook my head at him, smiling despite myself. Honestly, things might have been far worse. Evangeline had agreed to my offer of help, and while we had yet to figure out who'd murdered the vampire, everyone was on the same page. Provisionally.

"I prefer to only be visible to people who see me as more than a Reaper." Xavier took my hand, and his words made warmth spread to my core despite my lingering worries.

"I'll give you plenty of attention, then." I kissed him lightly. "What now?"

"I hoped to take you out to dinner," Xavier offered. "Unless you want to tell your family first?"

"There's not much to tell them." I glanced over at the pier, which remained cordoned off for the time being, and noted the absence of the crowds that had thronged the seafront over the weekend. "I hope Edwin reopens the pier soon. Estelle's already worried about people being put off returning to the carnival."

He followed my gaze to the pier. "I'm sure he will."

"Yeah, but Estelle is under a lot of pressure," I said. "The whole reason there were bits of wood everywhere is because a shifter threw a tantrum and smashed up a stall."

"A tantrum?" he echoed. "Never a dull moment, is there?"

"Nope." I indicated the Black Dog pub, our favourite hangout. "I'll text my aunt to let her know where we are. She won't mind."

"Good."

"Also, please tell me you're actually going to be visible to everyone when we walk in there," I added. "I don't want to look like I'm on a date with the invisible man."

"Of course." He chuckled in my ear as we walked arm in arm into the pub and picked out our favourite table. "I forgot to ask—is Estelle running the poetry night this evening?"

"You don't want to come, do you?" I asked. "I wanted to help Estelle to take some of the burden off her, but she insisted that my visit to Evangeline had earned me a pass."

"She's not wrong," he said. "I'd take a night with a bunch of amateur poets over a visit to the vampires, personally."

So would I, but this wasn't the first time I'd unwisely walked into a situation that most sane people would avoid. Still, the pub's cosy atmosphere did a fair job of soothing my nerves, even when it began to rain outside again.

"Not really the weather for a carnival," I remarked. "Might be for the best that they had a night off."

"We're glad too," said a passing bartender. "There were troublemakers all over the place last night."

"Troublemakers?" I echoed, thinking of the dead vampire. "In here?"

"Yeah, I had to throw out this drunken shifter who got really rowdy," he said. "He had these toy dragons he was trying to sell. Said his ex-wife wouldn't let him give them to their daughter."

"*That* guy?" I guessed his attempt to placate his daughter had not gone over well. To Xavier, I added, "That shifter was the one who caused a fuss yesterday. His kid turned into a wolf during a tantrum and nearly fell into the sea."

Despite my resolution to put the murder out of my mind, I had to admit that a drunken shifter could certainly have leapt at a vampire from behind. Vampires and shifters didn't get on at the best of times, either, and that guy had certainly had a short fuse—but Edwin would call that an assumption without proof. I'd keep that thought on the back burner for the time being.

"How pleasant," Xavier said dryly. "I see Estelle has her work cut out with the number of tourists in town, and so do the local bar staff."

"I don't think that guy was a tourist." When the bartender walked past our table again, I flagged him down. "Excuse me—I wondered if that shifter you threw out of the pub was a local?"

"Sure," he said. "I got his name—Patrick Jones—in case I needed to report him to the police. Any reason?"

"My cousin's running the carnival, and he's a known troublemaker there," I explained. "Also, did you hear about the guy who showed up dead this morning?"

"Yeah." His expression shuttered. "Nothing like a murder right on my doorstep to ruin the carnival mood."

"Was anyone working?"

He shook his head. "We'd already closed up for the night by then. Early hours of the morning, wasn't it?"

Right, of course. All the pubs would have closed at midnight, and even that shifter wouldn't have been on the seafront in the early hours. Still, it might be worth mentioning to Edwin.

As the bartender departed, I turned back to Xavier. "I'm inclined to think that guy died in a regular everyday scuffle, not a vampire conspiracy."

"I hope you're right," he said. "You don't need to give Evangeline more leverage over you."

"She already does. We made a bargain, remember? That was never going to go away on its own."

"I just worry about you." He spoke in a low voice. "I know I'm not the only one, but I'd be a lot happier if you kept me in the loop."

"I will, don't worry," I said. "What's the plan for your boss?"

"I'll try to let him down gently."

"He's the one who sent the vampire's soul to the afterlife," I said. "Would he know anything about how he died?"

"I can ask," he said. "I imagine he'd have told me if he did."

I raised a brow. "Are you sure?"

"I'll check," he said. "Regardless of his opinions on Evangeline, it'll cost him nothing to share."

I hoped so. I did not need to get myself indebted to another immortal. One was quite enough.

6

After a pleasant evening at the pub, Xavier walked me back to the library, where we caught the tail end of the poetry night. I felt bad for leaving Estelle to handle it alone, but she'd insisted that Xavier and I should enjoy ourselves.

After the last amateur poet had departed, Estelle and I were alone.

"So... how'd it go?" she asked.

"Which bit?" I asked. "My visit to update Edwin, or explaining my deal with Evangeline to Xavier?"

"The Grim Reaper didn't ambush your date, did he?"

"No, because Xavier hasn't told him yet," I said. "He's off to deliver the bad news. As for Edwin, he outright admitted he doesn't have any suspects yet, so I hope Evangeline isn't in a hurry for an update."

I made a mental note to double-check the locking spell on my room that night. I didn't want to wake up to her hovering over my bed like Sylvester had done this morning.

"I'm sure she'll play hard to get," said Estelle. "As for the

Grim Reaper... well, he already knew you were indebted to Evangeline."

"Yeah, he did." I heard a shuffling noise among the shelves and suspected a certain owl was eavesdropping on us. "How'd the poetry night go?"

She pulled a face. "Honestly, the kids I taught earlier were better at stringing a verse together than some of the locals. Might be my mood though."

"I should have come back sooner."

"Oh, it's not your fault. I think Aunt Candace would have been a hit if she'd agreed to do a reading, but you know how stubborn she is." She shook her head. "Anyway, I have another workshop tomorrow, but it isn't until the afternoon, so I can head to the beach in the morning to see if Edwin's willing to give the go-ahead to reopen the carnival."

"Speaking of the carnival," I said, "I spoke to one of the bartenders at the Black Dog, and he said that shifter whose kid threw a tantrum was being a nuisance at the pub, too, and ended up being kicked out."

"Oh, that guy?" she said. "I feel bad for the local bartenders. I hope he didn't cause too much of a hassle for them."

"No, but I'm wondering if there might be eyewitnesses to the vampire's murder who were in the pub too. Before it closed."

"At that hour in the morning? I doubt it," she said. "Doesn't Edwin have any leads?"

"He was trying to find out who the murder victim knew when he was alive," I explained. "The problem is that Evangeline made him cut off all contact with everyone."

"That's unfair of her."

"She probably thought she was doing him a favour," I

said. "I thought that maybe someone from his old life got irritated at him for running off to become a vampire."

That would be much easier than the Founders turning out to be involved. Or worse... Laney. "Isn't Laney up? Or is she avoiding the poetry night?"

Estelle followed my gaze to the corridor leading to our family's living quarters. "I think she's sleeping in. Or vampire equivalent."

"She did get woken up earlier." I'd rest easier if she stayed inside rather than going for any nocturnal wanders again. "I have to tell her though."

"Yeah." She walked with me to the living quarters, where I busied myself making us both mugs of hot cocoa in the kitchen while we waited for Laney to show herself.

Estelle and I settled on the sofa in the living room, and it wasn't long before the soft sound of quiet vampire footsteps announced my best friend's arrival.

"Hey, Rory." Laney entered the living room. "Hey, Estelle. Sorry I slept through the poetry night."

"You didn't miss much, believe me." Estelle sipped at her hot chocolate.

I put down my mug. "Do you have a vampire lesson tonight?"

"No... why?" she asked. "Evangeline didn't come back, did she?"

"Well... not exactly." I launched into an explanation of our arrangement after Edwin's visit to the library. It was easier than telling Xavier, but her eyes were as round as saucers by the time I'd finished.

"Why didn't you wake me up first?" she asked. "I could have gone with you as moral support."

"You already had to deal with Evangeline once today," I said. "Besides, I didn't know if she'd agree."

"Rory, I can't believe you went into her *office*," said Laney. "I'm pretty sure she never invites humans in there."

"I think she wanted to avoid eavesdroppers," I said. "Not sure why. It's not like she was sharing her deepest secrets."

"No, just the fact that someone murdered one of her own people, and she doesn't know who," she said. "What did Edwin say when he found out she said yes, then?"

"He was relieved, but he also doesn't have any suspects yet," I said. "Did you know the victim? Evangeline said he was new to being a vampire."

"No... I didn't know Jeffrey." She shrugged. "Like I told Evangeline, we've barely spoken three words to one another."

"I didn't know new vampires were that common." I glanced at Estelle, who'd leaned forwards in her seat to listen to Laney. "Doesn't Evangeline drill it into her recruits not to go around turning random humans into vampires at any opportunity?"

"Yeah, she does." Laney moved to an armchair, not quite meeting my eyes. "I have no idea who turned Jeffrey. He just showed up one day."

"He turned up on Evangeline's doorstep? Really?"

"That's the impression I got when I asked someone," she said. "Guess he figured throwing himself on her mercy was better than the alternative."

Namely, Evangeline hunting him down herself and strong-arming him into joining her. She'd done exactly that to Laney herself, and while Evangeline had taught her a lot, I was always aware that Laney's safety was entirely dependent upon the leading vampire's decision to spare her life. Oh, and her decision not to tell the other vampires that Laney had killed two of their own kind.

Realising I'd forgotten my hot chocolate, I scooped up my mug again before it went cold.

Laney shifted in her seat. "Rory... I don't know who killed that guy, but can you avoid telling Edwin that Evangeline questioned me about the murder?"

My grip on the mug tightened. "Why?"

"Because... well, I'm fairly sure Evangeline is the only person who knows I was responsible for the deaths of those two vampires who were allied with the Founders."

Meaning the ones that she'd killed to protect me. Evangeline knew, of course, and it was her protection that had ensured Laney had avoided a jail sentence. Not that jail was the worst possible fate. The other vampires would want a piece of her if they found out too. I'd forgotten even Edwin didn't know.

"I won't mention your name," I said. "Hopefully he'll come up with a decent list of suspects himself. It sounds like Evangeline forced the victim to cut off all contact with everyone in his former life, so there might be a few."

"Does he think it was someone Jeffrey knew before he turned?" she queried.

"He hasn't had a lot of time to make enemies among the vampires, so it's the logical guess."

As I put down my mug again, the lights cut out, plunging us into darkness. My heart jumped into my throat. "What...?"

The sound of thunder echoed in the background as if the storm had followed us into the library.

"It's only Cass." I heard the annoyance in Estelle's voice. "She's been doing that all evening."

"Doing what?" I asked, nonplussed. "Messing with the library?"

"Yeah, there's a reason I ended the poetry night early."

"You didn't tell me that."

"I wasn't going to mention it," said Estelle. "I'm pretty sure she's doing it because of your agreement with Evangeline. She's furious."

"Oh." I was doubly glad I'd gone out with Xavier for dinner instead of staying in the library. "Should have guessed."

"Maybe you should talk to her," said Laney's voice from the dark space opposite me.

"I probably ought to have told her myself, but it was hard enough explaining to Xavier."

"Xavier wasn't happy, then?" asked Laney.

"No, but he understands my choice."

His boss though? That was another issue, but I refused to let the case detonate my relationship with Xavier. If the murder was solved as quickly as possible, it didn't need to be an issue for the Grim Reaper.

On the other hand, Cass and I lived under the same roof. If she had a whole repertoire of tricks in store, as I suspected she did, then we were all in for a rough week.

∽

THE FOLLOWING MORNING, I woke up alone. No Xavier, but no Sylvester either. I'd barely slept thanks to Cass's antics the previous night, and there'd been no way to tell whether the incessant crackle of thunder and pounding raindrops had been real or a conjuration of the library's magic.

I could only assume my cousin had eventually tired herself out, as the library was mercifully dry and quiet while I took my time showering and dressing before heading downstairs. Estelle was nowhere to be seen, so I grabbed breakfast alone before heading to the morning's magic lesson with Aunt Candace.

As my aunt wasn't yet inside the classroom at the back of the library in which I took my lessons, I sat down to wait and pulled out my textbook, though there was no guarantee Aunt Candace's lecture of the day would cover anything relevant. It depended on her mood.

Several minutes passed before my aunt came walking into the room with a mug of coffee in her hand and my familiar perched on her shoulder. Jet flew over to my desk to greet me, while Aunt Candace eyed my textbook. "You won't be needing that today."

"Why not?" I asked warily.

"Because I'm going to teach you how to do something useful." She twirled her own wand in a snake-like manner, and a stream of musical notes drifted into the air.

"Whoa." I had to admit her display was pretty impressive. "How'd you do that?"

"With some very complicated magic that you're too much of a beginner to understand," she said. "If you want me to explain anyway, then I'll indulge you."

I regretted asking two minutes into a lecture that dragged on for half an hour until I'd lost all hope of ever being allowed to pick up my wand. When she noticed that I'd zoned out, she snapped her fingers.

"You aren't even trying to pay attention," she said. "Really. If I'm going to take time away from my manuscript for this, you can at least pretend to listen."

"Sorry, Aunt Candace," I said. "I'm just not sure how this is relevant."

Her eyes narrowed. "In that case, I'm going to test you on everything I just told you in our next lesson."

Honestly. "I'm just wondering when I'll get to practise the spell myself."

"Now, I thought you wanted to learn the theory first," she said. "One wrong note and you might put yourself to sleep by accident."

Your voice *is putting me to sleep,* I thought. Aloud, I said, "I don't even know *how* to do that. Can't you at least give another demonstration of how to cast the spell?"

She lifted her wand. "Certainly."

When she pointed the wand directly at me, I realised what she was about to do. "Wait—"

Too late. A flurry of musical notes echoed in my ears, and the next thing I knew, I was lying on my back, a concerned-looking Jet peering at my face.

"Huh." I blinked up at him. "Wait, where's Aunt Candace?"

"She left ten minutes ago, partner!"

"Honestly." I went to retrieve my textbook from the desk and found that my aunt had opened it onto a page that detailed how to cast the spell she'd just demonstrated. She'd also underlined a paragraph that said the spell was supposed to be effective against vampires as well as humans. Well, well.

Figuring the lesson wasn't a total loss after all, I made a mental note to practise the spell when I had a free moment later. Thanks to my unexpected nap, I'd missed the library's opening for the day, so I hurried to the front desk.

Throughout the morning, I did my level best to keep my attention on the job despite my internal debate as to whether Evangeline or Edwin would show up first. I hoped it would be the latter, but there were no guarantees, and it was anyone's guess as to whether Evangeline intended to keep me apprised of her own progress questioning her fellow vampires.

Then there was the question of how the Grim Reaper might have reacted yesterday when he'd learned the news. Since I'd received no messages from Xavier since the night before, it didn't take long before I started imagining worst-case scenarios. The Grim Reaper had told us that he wouldn't meddle in our relationship again, but making a deal with the head of the vampires might have been a step too far.

To avoid going too far down that train of thought, I volunteered to take a stack of books upstairs to the Magical Creatures Division. Since the books came equipped with sharp teeth, I had to wear gloves to handle them, and transporting them required all my attention if I wanted to avoid losing a finger. It wasn't until I'd reached the third floor that I remembered Cass was up here somewhere and given her shenanigans the previous night, she would not be thrilled to see me.

Unwilling to draw her attention, I moved quietly among the shelves, but the books were stored in a locked glass cabinet to keep them from biting any unwitting patrons, and it was impossible to move them without making a noise. The books snapped their teeth at me as I put them down on a stool so I could unlock the cabinet.

"Calm down," I muttered to them. "I'll only be a second."

The universe had other ideas. As I unlocked the cabinet, Aunt Adelaide's voice drifted up from the lobby. "Rory—Edwin's here."

I sprang away from the glass case, my gaze drifting towards the closed door to the corridor where Cass would be lurking. No doubt she'd heard every word, but there was no help for it. "Can you tell him I'll be a minute?"

I pulled open the cabinet door and put the books back into place as quickly as caution would allow and then fled the third floor before Cass had time to unleash another storm on me. I almost thought I'd escaped her wrath until I reached the stairs between the second and first floors and the top step promptly gave way beneath my feet, leaving me dangling over empty air.

"Thanks a bunch, Cass." I held on to the banister with my fingertips, trying to gain enough leverage to pull myself upright.

Sylvester flew past and laughed loudly at me. "Don't let go!"

"Very funny."

By the time I reached the lobby, I was sweating and frazzled, my hair sticking up in all directions and my clothes in disarray. Edwin looked slightly alarmed at the sight of me. "There you are, Rory."

"Hey, Edwin." I attempted to flatten my hair with my hand. "Do you have any updates for me?"

"You mean for Evangeline," he corrected. "Yes, potentially, but I'd prefer to avoid her knowing the names of the humans I want to question. Not before I can verify their innocence."

"I thought you were going to be open with her." I wiped the sweat from my brow with my sleeve. "Won't that make it easier for you to solve the case?"

"It's also my responsibility to prevent her from tormenting members of the public who have nothing to do with the murder," he said. "As no eyewitnesses have come forward, I'm being forced to build my list of suspects from the small number of people who the victim was acquainted with in his former life. For all I know, some of them might not even know he was a vampire given what you said of Evangeline persuading him to break contact with them."

Oh boy. I understood his reluctance to give the head vampire reason to unleash her anger on anyone who might turn out to be innocent, but if Evangeline figured out I was holding information back, it'd end badly for me, Edwin, *and* the person in question. Better to be straightforward with her.

"Who do you have in mind, then?" I asked. "Who's on your list?"

"The victim's family," he said. "He was already estranged from most of them when he turned, but his brother lives in Ivory Beach, so I've arranged a meeting with him. If you want to come with me, then you can."

I checked with my aunt first, who nodded. "Of course, Rory. Do tell me how it goes, won't you?"

"Of course," I said. "I'm not going to talk to Evangeline afterwards, but if she drops by and asks where I am..."

She winced. "Yes, I'll let her know."

"There's a ninety-five percent chance that she won't," I added. "This isn't really her time of day."

Yet I felt a twinge of guilt at my aunt's obvious discomfort, and while I had my family's full support, with the exception of Cass, I couldn't shake the feeling that I'd endangered them by agreeing to involve myself in this murder investigation. The sooner the killer was found, the better.

Edwin and I left the library, where two of his guards joined us. Being flanked by a pair of seven-foot-tall trolls was something of a reassurance, though I was pretty sure even they were no match for a vampire. Or the Grim Reaper, come to that.

Luckily, we saw neither of those as we walked across the

square and partway up the high street before veering down a side road. Edwin led the way to an apartment block and rang the buzzer. A few moments later, a middle-aged guy dressed in a tracksuit answered the door, looking as if he'd just woken up. His greying hair was rumpled, and his eyes were bloodshot.

"Hey, Edwin," he said. "Sorry, it's a mess in here... I don't normally entertain guests."

He wasn't kidding, as I found out when I followed Edwin into the singularly messiest room I'd ever set eyes on. Junk food wrappers and bottles littered every surface, while the sofa smelled as if someone had spilled beer all over it. I didn't sit down, instead hovering awkwardly near the door while Edwin questioned the man. "When was the last time you saw your brother, Jonas?"

"We hadn't spoken in months," Jonas said. "Did you say he was a vampire now? Really?"

"How did you not know that about your own brother?" The question escaped before I could think better of it. After all, I knew not everyone was close to their family members even though I'd grown so used to living in the library with the others. That didn't mean none of us kept secrets, either, Cass being an obvious example. The thought of her as a vampire was a frightening one. She was scary enough as a witch, let alone an immortal.

Not that "immortal" necessarily meant "undying," as Jeffery's fate had proven.

"Like I said. We weren't close." He rubbed his eyes with the back of his hand. "He was more ambitious than I am. Wanted to get a good job. Can't think how he fell in with that crowd."

"What crowd?" I knew I was supposed to leave the questioning to Edwin, but the word "crowd" conjured the memory of the way Laney had been unwittingly drawn into the magical world via the Founders.

"Evangeline's lot." He gave a shudder. "Dunno how anyone can voluntarily spend time with them. Creeps, all of them."

As far as I could judge, his reaction was genuine. He certainly wasn't a vampire, and he didn't look athletic enough to stab one of them in the back.

"All right," Edwin said. "Do you know anyone your brother might have kept in touch with?"

"Yeah, there was this guy he was dating when we last spoke to one another," he said. "I thought things were going well, but if Jeffrey broke off contact with him after he turned, then I guess not."

"Can you give me his details?" asked Edwin.

"His name's Eric Tanner... and I think he lives down by the seafront."

A few minutes later, Edwin and I left the building and joined the trolls. They'd waited outside, as they were unable to fit under the door frame.

"We're going to see this Eric guy now?" I asked Edwin.

"I suppose we are," he said grudgingly. "I don't need to reiterate that this is an exception to the usual procedure for investigating a crime."

"No, you don't," I said. "Really. I don't want to work for the police. I just want the vampires off my back."

"So say we all."

As we walked back to the high street, I glanced uphill towards the spired roofs of the church where the vampires lived.

"Do you think I should tell her?" I asked Edwin. "About our chat with Jeffrey's brother?"

"Definitely not," he said. "Nothing about our conversation suggested Jonas was actively involved enough in his brother's life to have killed him. I can't say I understand Jeffrey's reasoning in cutting off contact with his former acquaintances, but I imagine you might."

"Not exactly." I hadn't had much to lose when I'd left the normal world behind, and I'd ultimately ended up bringing my sole close friend along with me into the magical world— albeit by accident. "If you mean Laney, then I don't know whether she misses her old life. She and her parents aren't close."

Considering their reaction when she'd come out as a lesbian as a teenager, I could only imagine how they'd react if she admitted she drank blood to survive. Not that we were technically *allowed* to share anything about the magical world with outsiders. Jeffery, at least, had lived here in Ivory Beach prior to being turned into a vampire.

"Regardless, this Eric might prove a more promising lead," said Edwin. "It's unlikely that Jeffrey would have withheld that information from someone he was romantically involved with."

"You never know," I said. "Depends how insistent Evangeline was that he cut off all contact with his previous life."

It didn't make Evangeline seem any more endearing, I'd say that much. Her allowing Laney to stay in the library was a surprisingly generous offer, by her standards.

Laney's comment from the previous night came to mind, and I resolved to refrain from mentioning her name again in front of Edwin. He might not know she'd killed those two vampires—and the responsibility for them was technically Evangeline's anyway—but it wouldn't do anything but create unnecessary friction between us.

Better to keep that quiet... and hope that Eric had more to share than Jonas had.

7

Edwin and I walked down to the seafront, flanked by his troll guards, where we found Eric's home down a short cul-de-sac off the road that ran parallel to the beach. Edwin knocked on the door to the modest terraced house, which opened to reveal a dishevelled man with red-rimmed eyes and a nervous tremor in his hands. If I had to guess, he'd heard the news of Jeffrey's tragic death. No surprise given how close he lived to the seafront... and the crime scene.

"You're with the police." He blinked at Edwin then spotted me standing behind him. "You aren't though."

"Aurora is assisting me," said Edwin. "If you don't mind, I'd like to come in and ask you a few questions."

His mouth pulled down at the corners. "I guess you can come in."

Mercifully, Eric's house was relatively clean compared to Jonas's messy bachelor pad. Edwin and I sat on the sofa in the small living room, while Eric hovered in the kitchen doorway. "I... sorry, why are you here?"

"I think you know." Edwin kept his tone kind, but there

was a note of steel beneath it that I'd never heard from him before. "I'm here to ask about your relationship with Jeffery."

Eric flinched. "We don't have one. He cut me off."

"Former relationship, then," he said. "I assume you heard he was found dead yesterday."

He nodded, eyes shining with tears. "Yeah."

"That's why I wanted to talk to you," Edwin said gently. "I know it's unpleasant for you to remember, but we want to find out who was responsible for what happened to him."

Eric sat down in an armchair and wiped his eyes on the back of his hand. "You don't think I had anything to do with his death… do you?"

"It's my job to question anyone with a connection to the victim," he said. "Due to his estrangement from his former life, it's proven challenging, so I hope you'll cooperate with me."

"He turned into a vampire and left me," he choked. "Now it turns out he's dead. Surely one of *them* is the culprit."

"Did you know he was a vampire?" I asked curiously.

"Yes, of course I did." He lowered his gaze. "He came back and told me after—after he turned. He said that he was ending things with me, and that he'd be living with the vampires from now on."

Harsh. Had Eric been heartbroken enough to literally stab him in the back though? I didn't know.

"So that was the last time you spoke," said Edwin. "You haven't seen him since?"

"No," said Eric. "I haven't even been to the carnival. I don't get out much these days."

Hmm. He sounded sincere enough, but without a

vampire's mind-reading talent, I couldn't make any definite judgements. Neither could Edwin.

"Who else did he regularly see before he turned?" asked Edwin. "I found out your name from his brother, but it's otherwise been difficult for me to find his acquaintances."

"Oh, Jonas," Eric said. "I forgot he was even still living here in Ivory Beach. They didn't see each other that often."

"I gathered," Edwin said. "Do you know of anyone else who he was in contact with prior to being turned into a vampire?"

"No... I mean, there was his old workplace, but he got laid off a few months ago," he said. "I figured that was why he started spending time around the vampires. I wish he'd *told* me." He blinked hard, fighting to hold back the tears.

"It would help to have the details of that workplace, in case I need them later on," said Edwin. "Do you know?"

Eric gave him the address, while I scanned the room in the futile hopes of picking up on a clue that might point to a link with the vampires. The living room, though, was ordinary enough to be almost generic, from the flatscreen TV mounted on the wall to the sports paraphernalia in the glass cabinets. My examination led me to conclude that Eric was a fan of the magical game called Sky Hopper, but not that he'd met with any vampires recently. He certainly wasn't one himself.

"I wish I could tell you more," Eric added. "Jeffrey wasn't really sociable, so it was weird that he started going out at night, but I never... never expected anything like this."

"We'll do our best to find out who did this," Edwin said as we stood up to leave. "I'll be in touch if I need to speak to you again."

When we left the house and the door closed behind us, I

turned to Edwin. "You're going to talk to his former employers?"

"I'll try," he said, "but it's looking as if it'll be a dead end given that he left long before he became a vampire."

"Maybe Evangeline had more luck." Given our chat yesterday, I had my doubts though. If we'd already hit the extent of Edwin's suspect list, though, where else was there to go? I racked my mind and recalled my conversation with the bartender at the Black Dog the previous day. "Edwin, have you asked for eyewitnesses to come forward?"

He gave me a strange look. "Yes, but I don't think there were many people wandering around the pier at five in the morning. Why?"

"I spoke to one of the bartenders at the Black Dog yesterday who said that some of the people who went to the carnival might have stuck around after closing time," I explained. "Maybe one of them saw something."

"That's a little too vague for me to do anything with." He continued to walk alongside the seafront, where I spotted a growing throng of people near the end of the pier. By the looks of things, the carnival's attractions were in the process of reopening. Sure enough, I spotted Estelle talking to someone near the end of the pier.

When she saw us approaching, she hurried over and smiled at me. "Hey, Rory. Hey, Edwin."

"Hey," I said. "You're allowed to reopen the event, then?"

"Yes," Edwin answered. "I gave the go-ahead this morning since we don't need any more disruption in the middle of the tourist season."

"I know," said Estelle. "I hope the incident won't put off our visitors, but the weather's looking up."

"It is." A few people were even sunbathing on the beach, as was typical whenever a single ray of sunshine showed itself. As Edwin returned to the police station with his troll guards flanking him, I added, "I take it he already had enough of a look around the crime scene?"

"There wasn't much to look at." She gestured at the sandy hill near where we'd seen the body floating in the water. The tide had shifted, so no doubt any clues that might have been left behind would have long since been washed away. "Please don't walk into the sea, Rory. I'd prefer not to have to fish you out."

"I won't." Xavier was the one who could walk into the water and not get wet, let alone drown. "Why would I do that?"

"Okay, that's more Aunt Candace's sort of thing."

"Or Cass, when she was regularly meeting up with her kelpie," I added. "Have you seen *her* today?"

"No," she said. "I hope she isn't terrifying any visitors at the library with another thunderstorm."

I groaned. "Typical. We were almost getting along over the weekend when Xavier came over, so I hoped she'd started to mellow a little."

"Well, yeah, but that was before..."

"Before Evangeline, I know." I was starting to wonder if I ought to confront Cass face-to-face to get it over with, but the idea appealed about as much as another visit to the vampires' church. "That's another reason I wish we'd made more progress on the investigation."

"None of Edwin's leads panned out, then?"

"Nope." I gave the pier another scan, my gaze lingering on the stall with the cuddly dragons. The frame that had been destroyed in the shifter's rampage appeared to have been replaced with a new one, and the remaining plush dragons swayed gently in the breeze. "Did someone already win the replacements for those toys?"

"Huh?" Estelle followed my gaze. "No, we haven't reopened any of the attractions yet. The guy running that stall has taken the day off."

"Ah." Wait. I could have sworn I saw movement behind the wooden frame, as someone ducked out of sight. "Then who's that?"

"Is someone there?" When no answer came, Estelle's expression hardened. A simple flick of her wand unearthed the shifter who'd been causing trouble the previous weekend, who yelped when she levitated him into the air. "Let me go!"

"What were you doing hiding behind there?" I indicated the stall, bemused. "Didn't you already win enough cuddly dragons?"

He didn't reply, but a distinct jangling noise came from his pockets as he continued to fight Estelle's levitation spell.

"You were stealing from the money box," said Estelle. "Weren't you?"

"No," he said. "No, I don't know what you're talking about."

"First you cheated to win about five of those dragons, now this?" Estelle flicked her wand again, depositing him on the ground. "Put it back. Every penny."

He slunk over to the stall, digging his hands in his pockets and muttering curses under his breath. What had possessed him to try stealing right in front of the police station? Had he known Edwin wasn't in?

In fact... what if this wasn't the only crime he'd committed?

"You should report him to Edwin," I whispered to Estelle. "The police already have his name, according to the bartender at the Black Dog."

She shook her head. "It's not worth bothering. The

carnival opens properly in less than an hour, and I need to be focused."

"Don't you tell tales on me," the shifter growled, overhearing. "You can have the money back. I don't care.

He upended his wallet on the ground, and coins scattered everywhere. While Estelle and I ran to collect them, he seized the chance to slink away.

"Don't, Rory," Estelle insisted when I made for the police station. "Edwin already has enough on his mind. I'll ask him if he can spare any of his trolls to keep an eye out here when we reopen. That ought to put that guy off coming back."

"If you're sure." I helped her gather up the scattered coins and return them to the box, which Estelle locked securely. "I ought to go back to the library to help your mum."

Aunt Adelaide must be running the place alone since her sister and daughter rarely lifted a finger, and the latter was an ongoing force of terror at the moment. Crossing my fingers behind my back that I wouldn't return to another of Cass's thunderstorms, I headed back to the library.

When I opened the door, I thought nobody was at the front desk at first. Then I heard the sound of a pen scratching in the background.

"Aunt Candace, I can hear you," I said. "If you want an update on the investigation, I don't have much to say."

"Tell me anyway." She popped up from behind the stacks with an expectant look on her face, her notebook and pen hovering at her side.

"Only if you give me a hand with the returns."

We haggled for a bit—making an agreement with Aunt Candace was almost as tricky as negotiating with Evangeline—before she reluctantly agreed to take any returns up to the Magical Creatures Division so I wouldn't have to risk running into another of Cass's pranks.

When I'd finished telling her about our chat with Eric—and the encounter with the shifter at the beach—she tutted. "Pity. I could have come up with a more interesting list of suspects."

"I'm sorry my real-life murder investigation isn't exciting enough for one of your books." I rolled my eyes at her. "If it's any consolation, I'm annoyed, too, especially as I have to tell Evangeline whenever she asks me for an update."

"I'm sure she can shake answers out of the suspects herself." She bared her teeth in a grin that was worthy of Evangeline herself. "Especially that would-be thief who tried to steal from Estelle."

"I never said that guy was a suspect for the murder." He'd demonstrated a quick temper in the couple of times I'd seen him, but I couldn't picture him having the patience to sneak up on a vampire from behind.

"He should be," she said. "I think I'll give him a special death in my next book as punishment."

"Feel free." At least she hadn't decided to involve herself directly in the investigation, but I did need to give a meaningful update to Evangeline, if I could think of one that wouldn't end in her visiting either of the people we'd spoken to. Pity we didn't know where that shifter lived, really. What had the bartender said his name was again? Patrick? Suspect or not, he had some nerve trying to steal from Estelle right in front of the police, but that didn't make him a murderer.

I didn't hear from Xavier until the library had closed for the day. As I was tidying the front desk, a knock on the door made my shoulders tense for a moment before I remembered Evangeline wouldn't feel the need to knock. Neither should Xavier, really, but when I opened the door, I found him waiting on the other side.

"Hey." I greeted him with a customary hug, which he returned with what I thought was less enthusiasm than usual. I might have been imagining things, though, given my worries about how the Grim Reaper had reacted to the news that I'd made a deal with his immortal enemy.

"Hey." Xavier gave me a smile that banished some of my nerves. "Sorry I haven't been around. I figured you'd be out, helping Edwin to question people."

"You told your boss, then?" I asked. "So... what did the Grim Reaper have to say?"

"Not much," he said. "He said if the vampires want to get into a scuffle with the police over the murder of one of their own, then it's not my problem to deal with."

"Really?" I frowned. "That's it? He didn't mention me?"

"He advised me not to get involved in the investigation, but he didn't explicitly forbid me from talking to you about it."

"Weird." Or rather, too good to be true. "Isn't he even bothered that I'm helping Evangeline?"

"He knew that you owed her a favour," he said. "Like you said yourself, there's a lot worse you might have done to fulfil that bargain."

"I did say that." I certainly hadn't expected the Grim Reaper to agree though. "That's a nice change."

"Isn't it?" He studied my face. "Are you okay though?"

"Just a bit frustrated," I admitted. "I hoped to have made more progress by now. Our leads were kind of a bust. I figured Evangeline might have had more luck."

"You haven't seen her today?"

"Evangeline?" I lowered my voice. "Not yet, but I don't think we ever explicitly agreed on a time for me to update her. I'd like to avoid her visiting the library again, though, since Cass is already in a foul mood."

"Then you want to talk to her in person."

"I don't *want* to, but it's better than the alternative." Meaning her swooping into the library when I wasn't expecting her. "Have you ever seen the inside of Evangeline's home?"

"There aren't many places I haven't seen," he said. "I can walk through walls, remember?"

"You've even been in *there*?"

"I got curious when I became an apprentice Reaper," he said. "Granted, that was a few years ago."

"It looked surprisingly normal to me. No hidden corpses or torture instruments or anything."

"Don't even, Rory," he said. "Frankly, I'm surprised she invited you into her house at all."

"It's not the first time, remember?" I told him. "Not that I want a repeat of that party, in any capacity."

His expression darkened. He hadn't been present at the party himself, the one that had ended in the death of a vampire, but he remembered the aftermath as clearly as I did.

"Evangeline doesn't, either, I'd wager," I added. "She's angry enough at losing one of her people that she's willing to cede some authority, even if she won't admit so directly, but I'm not sure she'll be impressed with my update."

"You could do with a couple more clues from her, right?" he asked. "It doesn't sound like she gave you much information on the victim. Did she even mention who turned the guy into a vampire?"

"Come to think of it, no." Why hadn't I thought of that? "I should have asked."

I'd been surprised to learn that the victim was new to

being a vampire, but the question of who'd turned him had somehow never crossed my mind. That might be a route worth pursuing.

"Are you sure you want to go there tonight?" His brow creased. "You can wait."

"I'm sure." I sought out Aunt Adelaide, who was tidying the Reading Corner and who reacted to my explanation with a resigned nod.

"Better to take Xavier with you, I think," she advised. "I'll breathe easier when this is done."

"Same here, believe me."

After leaving the library, I crossed the square, walking hand in hand with Xavier. As we walked, I told him about our visits to Jonas and then to Eric.

"I'm not sure I should mention them to Evangeline," I said to him as we neared the church. "They didn't seem guilty, and they don't deserve a visit from her."

Maybe I needed to give Evangeline the benefit of the doubt though. When she'd invited me into her home, she hadn't done me any harm, and unless you counted her barbed comment directed at my relationship with Xavier, she hadn't even tried to manipulate me. While I ran the risk of her making a similar comment with Xavier himself present this time, it did make me feel more secure to have him at my side as we approached the church. It wasn't dark yet, but the vampires would have woken by this hour, and the feeling of being watched hung over me as I knocked on the door.

Evangeline answered, and she raised a brow when she saw Xavier at my side. "Aurora. I assume you have an update for me?"

"I do." I gave her a rundown of my visits with Edwin,

though I refrained from directly mentioning the addresses of the people we'd questioned.

"Is that all?" she said when I was finished. "You've made no progress at all?"

"I don't think either of the people we've spoken to are likely contenders for murder, but there might be eyewitnesses at the beach..." I trailed off, knowing my vagueness annoyed her.

"If that's all you have to say, then I bid you good night," she said. "I hope that you have more to tell me tomorrow."

"Wait," I said. "Ah—have *you* made any progress today? Have you identified any suspects?"

Her brow twitched. "Edwin wants to know, does he?"

"No." Xavier's presence likely wouldn't convince her to be open with me, so I'd have to get her alone. "I just thought that we could put our ideas together. We can talk inside, if you like."

"What is the reason for your curiosity, Aurora?" Irritation underlaid her tone. "Please cease avoiding the subject that is on your mind."

Nothing for it. "I wondered—who turned Jeffery into a vampire?"

Her eyes narrowed. "That's irrelevant."

"Are you sure?" I suppressed a flinch at her severe expression, though I couldn't think what had prompted such a hostile reaction. "It might be relevant. I mean—he was turned recently, after all, and that's not common, is it?"

"Yes, I'm sure." She didn't answer my question, I noticed. "You may leave."

I watched the door close behind her, feeling slightly wrong-footed.

"What was that about?" I muttered to Xavier. "Why not tell me? Unless she turned him herself?"

"I doubt it," he said. "I'm not the mind reader though."

"Nor me." I turned my back on the vampires' home. "If she won't tell me now, then I'll have to wait for her to change her mind."

Or ask Laney.

8

Xavier walked me back to the library, and we reluctantly parted ways on the doorstep. As I entered, I spotted Laney's graceful approach from the living quarters.

"Hey, Rory," she said.

"Hey," I said. "You're not going out, are you?"

"I have a lesson with Evangeline." She grimaced. "I don't want to get on her bad side again."

"Is that a good idea?" I queried. "She's only just taken you off her suspect list. If I were you, I'd want to avoid her."

"I can't skip out on my lesson, or she'll have even more reason to believe I have something to hide."

"I'd have thought she'd be too busy to run classes," I remarked. "Not that she's telling *me* anything, mind. I don't suppose you know who turned Jeffrey into a vampire?"

"Huh?" She blinked at me, another unconscious habit from her human life. "No, why?"

"Evangeline wouldn't tell me, so I wondered if anyone else knew," I explained. "She claimed it's irrelevant to the investigation into his death, but I get the feeling that she's holding out on me."

"I can poke around and see if I can find out," she offered.

"Please don't risk yourself for my sake," I said hastily. "If Evangeline thinks I've put you up to it, she's even more likely to retaliate."

"I won't take any risks," she said. "I can peek into a few minds without saying a word aloud. I'll be careful."

That didn't mean the other vampires would be pleased if they figured out that she was poking around in their heads, but from the little Laney had told me of the time she'd spent around them outside of lessons, they did that kind of thing to one another all the time. Feuds had sprung up entirely because someone had stumbled across the wrong secret or delved into the mind of someone who didn't appreciate the intrusion. Evangeline's own mind was off-limits, but some of the others seemed to make a sport of seeing what scandalous information they could unearth.

I couldn't accompany Laney to her vampire lesson without inviting questions, so I stayed up to wait for her return. Since Estelle had her hands full with the carnival and my aunt had opted for an early night, I stayed downstairs on the sofa with my dad's journal in a bid to keep myself from dozing off. With difficulty because I'd hit a stretch of journal entries that were meandering enough to make even Aunt Candace yawn and put the book down. Since I had to translate each page individually, there was little I could do but push onwards until I reached an interesting stretch. There were a few fun moments in there, such as my dad's fond recollections of the mischief I'd got up to as an infant, but he hadn't mentioned any encounters with the magical world for a while.

Or the Founders. I knew the vampires must have been

on his mind even so, as he'd unwittingly claimed a valuable book from their clutches and then left it with the Grim Reaper for safekeeping. It wasn't long before my attention began to wander back to my own vampire-related dilemmas, though, and I found myself watching the clock, impatient for Laney to return.

Whether Laney found out any pertinent information or not, there was nothing to suggest Jeffrey's death had been anything other than a regular everyday argument that had gotten out of hand... but why would Evangeline refuse to admit who'd turned him into a vampire?

What else might she be hiding?

∼

"Rory," whispered a voice.

I blinked awake, disorientated. I'd fallen asleep on the sofa, my dad's journal beside me, and the dim light of the lamp on the table coupled with my grogginess meant that I assumed the voice had come from Laney until I properly opened my eyes and saw...

"Whoa." I jumped upright. "Cass... what are you doing?"

"What?" She looked insulted at my reaction. "I'm waking you up. No need to act as if I stabbed you with a red-hot poker."

I might have pointed out that given her fury over my arrangement with Evangeline, I was justified in being slightly alarmed to find her leaning over me—but another question came to mind. "Why did you wake me up?"

"Because," she said through gritted teeth, "there's a vampire in the library. And it's not Laney."

Her pronouncement had me on my feet in a second. "What?"

"Keep it down," she hissed. "Whoever it is, they're over by the research section."

"What...?" Questions cascaded through my mind as I struggled to shake off my sleepiness. Where were the others? Why had she woken me and not called Sylvester?

"Now's not the time for you to be slow to catch on." She paced out of the living room, clutching her wand in her hand. "If you aren't going to help, then stay out of the way."

Why had she woken me in the first place? Cass's expression was serious enough that she surely couldn't be pulling my leg, so I reached into my pocket for my Biblio-Witch Inventory before following her out of the living room and into the lobby.

Lanterns hovered above our heads and cast warm orange lights across the shelves, but darkness cloaked the area behind the front desk. I strained my ears and heard the distinct sound of soft footfalls as Cass and I neared the shadowy stacks.

Holding my Biblio-Witch Inventory in one hand, I ran my fingertips down the topmost page and tapped the word *light*.

A dazzling glow bloomed from my hand, bathing the entire right-hand side of the library in whiteness. There, the intruder's shadow appeared frozen against a bookshelf.

"Who are you?" Cass demanded.

The woman simply gaped at us like a moth caught in the fire of a lantern, her eyes wide and staring. Cass was right. A vampire had got into the library. *How?*

"Did Laney let you in?" I asked. It didn't make the intrusion any less alarming, but it was better than a total stranger breaking in to do us harm.

The vampire flushed. "Ah... yes?"

Cass pointed her wand at the vampire. The woman

yelped, flying head over heels, and crashed into a heap in front of the shelves. She lay twitching and moaning, her limbs akimbo.

"Wait..." Now I looked closer, she didn't move like a vampire would, and she was visibly trembling with none of her previous stillness. Despite the stealthy manner in which she'd entered the library, she was human.

Cass ignored me and pointed her wand at the woman. "You'll pay for breaking in."

I grabbed her arm. "She's not a vampire."

"Yes, she is. No regular person moves that quietly."

"A vampire would have run by now."

Yes, the intruder had been abnormally stealthy, but I'd seen that trait in humans before. Specifically, humans who'd been drinking vampire blood. Like Laney had before she'd turned into one of them.

"Whatever she is, she shouldn't be here." Cass fired off a freeze-frame spell that caused the woman to halt midmotion. Then she stalked over to the desk, where she ducked out of sight before emerging with a rope from the drawer in which we kept the tools to restrain rowdy books.

Cass secured the intruder's hands behind her back before dragging her past the stacks. Over her shoulder, she said, "I didn't give permission for your friend to bring one of her chew toys in here."

"I don't think Laney actually invited her in." Vampires might not be able to enter anyone's home without an invitation, but the library was open to the public, as Evangeline occasionally liked to remind me. "Where's Sylvester?"

"That," said Cass, "is a very good question."

A shiver ran down my spine. *Where is everyone?*

"My mother and sister are probably asleep," she added, presumably sensing my thoughts. "And Aunt Candace never notices anything anyway. Sylvester, though... what did you do with him, eh?"

The woman didn't answer, letting Cass drag her through the stacks without resistance.

A thumping noise came from behind a nearby classroom door, and I halted, spinning on my heel. "Wait. Someone's in there."

The door appeared to be locked, so I opened my Biblio-Witch Inventory again and tapped the word *unlock*.

Sylvester exploded out of the door with a shriek of anger that echoed all the way up to the library's ceiling. The woman screamed when the giant owl landed on her head, his claws digging in.

"Whoa." I sprang back, and even Cass let go of the intruder to avoid her bare skin being snagged in the owl's claws.

"How dare you disrespect me!" Sylvester screeched, his beak perilously close to taking one of her tightly closed eyes out.

"Don't peck her to death before we can find out why she came here," I told him. "Tone it down. We need answers."

"Yes, we do." Cass, to my surprise, shooed Sylvester away and grabbed the intruder's shoulders before shoving her through the door into the deserted classroom. "Go on, talk. Otherwise, I'll lock you *and* the owl in here together."

The woman burst into tears, loud sobs that echoed in the empty room, and covered her face with her hands.

"Oh, come on." Cass looked disgusted at the very sight of her.

"I'll give her something to cry about." Sylvester flew at the classroom again.

"Wait." I held up a hand to hold him back. "Give her the

chance to tell us why she broke into the library before you start terrorising her, Sylvester."

The woman continued to sob, so I walked past Cass and into the room, motioning to the others to stay back before I addressed the would-be vampire. "Why are you here? Do you even know Laney?"

"No." She whimpered, hands covering her face. "I don't mean any of you harm."

"But I bet your vampire master does." Cass's words dripped with venom. "Is it true?"

"Did someone send you here?" I asked the woman. "Why?"

She gave another whimper. "To steal a book. That's all."

"A book?" My dad's journal came to mind first, followed by the book he'd obtained from the Founders, and my blood ran cold. "Tell me which book."

"A—a book of vampire lore."

My spine stiffened. *That book.* My dad had obtained the book of vampire lore without realising the danger of possessing something the Founders desired, and when he'd realised that they were willing to kill to get their hands on it, he'd handed the book to the Grim Reaper for safekeeping. The book had then passed to Evangeline before she'd handed it back to the library. A surprising act of generosity, or so it had seemed at the time... but if this woman had come on behalf of the Founders, then word had reached them somehow.

Cass grabbed my arm and yanked me out of the room before slamming the door on the intruder. "I'd say we put it to a vote on what we should do with her. How about feeding her to the things in the Nightmares Section?"

"What is going on?" Aunt Adelaide walked into view,

clad in a flowery dressing gown, and eyed the classroom door. "Is someone in there?"

"We had a break-in," Sylvester informed her. "A vampire came to steal from us and had the audacity to assault me."

"Not a vampire," I corrected him. "She was working for them, though, and she came to steal the book of vampire lore. The one my dad had."

"*That* book?" Estelle joined her mother, her expression aghast. "I'm sorry. I should have been listening for intruders, but I was so tired."

"She locked Sylvester in the classroom so he wouldn't give her away." I indicated the door. "I'm not sure she knew where to find the book. I don't know where it is."

In fact, I was pretty certain Sylvester was the only person who *did* know the book's current location, though he'd never have shared it with a stranger.

"Amateur or not, she still managed to break in," said Cass. "That means we have to punish her... and your friend too."

"You know she's not Laney's friend—or chew toy," I added. "She's here because someone *else* sent her, and I'd like to know who that is, wouldn't you?"

"Yes," said Estelle. "If she's looking for *that* book, then who is she answering to? Not the Founders?"

"Likely yes," said Aunt Adelaide grimly. "She can't stay in here."

"I know, but I'm pretty sure feeding her to the Nightmares Section is breaking the law." I gave Cass a pointed look. "And so is letting Sylvester peck her to death."

"She's halfway to death already," the owl said.

"Cass didn't hit her that hard, did she?"

"That's not what he means." Cass reached for the door handle. "I thought there was something odd about her..."

"Aside from the obvious?" I tensed when she opened the classroom door, ready to stop Sylvester from dive-bombing our prisoner, and saw that the woman had retreated into a corner, her arms over her face.

"Tell me everything about who sent you here," Cass demanded. "Now."

"Start with your name." I joined my cousin, while the others crowded into the room behind us.

"Diane," she said shakily. "You're not going to kill me... are you?"

"We're deciding," said Cass, with a wicked grin. "Right now, we're debating whether to let our owl peck you to death, or whether to throw you into the Nightmares section instead."

"Cass." Aunt Adelaide walked in front of her daughter and spoke to the intruder. "Diane, I'd appreciate it if you could tell me who sent you here."

"I... can't." She choked on the words. "I can't. I'm sworn not to tell anyone..."

"Maybe I can loosen your tongue." Cass made to enter the room, but Estelle grabbed her arm and restrained her. Undeterred, Cass pushed on. "I know you've been drinking their blood, so you're less fragile than you look."

"Can't you..." The woman gulped. "Can't you just call the police instead?"

She had a point, but Evangeline was usually the first port of call for a rogue vampire situation, and she wouldn't be thrilled if I told Edwin instead of her. Though the reverse was true as well. If we handed her to Evangeline, we'd lose our chance to get a full explanation as to what she was doing in the library.

"Someone died recently," I said to the woman. "A local vampire. Know anything about that?"

She shook her head frantically. "No. I've never even been here before."

"Really," Aunt Adelaide said. "Then where are you from? Who sent you here?"

The woman blinked a couple of times, and then she slumped against the wall, apparently in a dead faint.

"She's faking," said Cass.

"I don't think she is." I walked across the classroom, while Aunt Adelaide entered the room behind me. "You probably terrified the living daylights out of her."

Cass broke free of Estelle's hold. "That or she's about to turn. I won't have another of *them* in the library. Not again."

My heart lurched. "What... you don't think one of the vampires already bit her?"

"That's what I meant by being at death's door, you doorknob," came Sylvester's petulant voice. "Pity. I would have enjoyed finishing her off myself."

Crouching down, I checked Diane's pulse... and found none. I recoiled, reminded of when Laney had fallen into a coma after being bitten and had awoken as one of the undead. Whether the people who'd sent her here had intended for her to undergo the transformation here and now was debatable, but two things were clear.

The Founders were recruiting again, and they'd officially made a move against us.

9

I rose to my feet, dread ballooning inside my chest. We couldn't keep the soon-to-be vampire here. We had to hand her over to Evangeline.

When I voiced this aloud, not everyone agreed with my plan. Cass and Sylvester both wanted the vampire brought to a permanent end before she reawakened, while Aunt Adelaide and Estelle disagreed. Our argument lasted several minutes before the noise finally woke up Aunt Candace, who came flying downstairs at such speed that her notebook and pen nearly knocked Sylvester out of the air.

His indignant hooting was loud enough that it was a wonder the vampire didn't wake up. Covering my ears, I backed away from the furious owl and stumbled when my feet caught against the rim of a trapdoor.

"Cass, was that you?" I indicated the trapdoor, which led into the basement where the library's *other* resident vampire lay in a seemingly permanent slumber. "Were you going to put our prisoner in there?"

The vampire in the basement had been a fixture since long before I'd moved into the library, and my grandmother hadn't told any of her children about his presence before her death. As a result, nobody even knew his name. Over the past few months, I'd progressed from curiosity about the mysterious man who slept in a coffin beneath our feet to forgetting he existed, like the rest of my family members. If he ever woke up, it might not be for a hundred years or more.

"No, I assume it's the library's idea of a joke," Cass answered. "We don't need to give Evangeline another ally. We have to take care of her permanently before she wakes up."

"She's not going to wake up," I pointed out. "Not for several days, in fact, which means we have time to decide who to hand her over to in the meantime."

"Certainly not," said Aunt Adelaide. "As soon as she wakes up, she'll want fresh blood, and there's no telling how long the process will take. We ought to call the police. If Edwin agrees that she ought to face the consequences for breaking onto our property, he'll find somewhere to keep her where she won't be a danger to anyone."

"I know how to stake a vampire, if need be," added Cass.

"We need to find out everything about whoever sent her here," I said. "Or at the very least get her into the hands of someone who'd be as interested to know as the rest of us."

"Meaning Evangeline." Cass's jaw twitched. "I don't appreciate this, Rory. I don't care how badly you wanted to repay your debt. You didn't need to drag the rest of us into it too."

"This has nothing to do with me."

"It was your dad's book she was looking for."

I grimaced. She was right on that one, but it'd been weeks since I'd taken the book from Evangeline, and I couldn't think what had prompted the timing of the break-in. Diane couldn't be linked to the vampire who'd been murdered, not if she wasn't local. Right?

Estelle came to my defence. "Would you rather the Founders had the book? Besides, Evangeline gave it to us."

"Her again." She scoffed. "Fine. Have it your way. We'll take our prisoner straight to the vampires' home and hope that Evangeline deals with the problem. Permanently."

"What—now?" Laney wasn't in the library, though her vampire lesson would be long over by this hour. "Don't you want to wait until Laney comes back so we can ask for her advice?"

"If your friend has an objection, then you can tell her she shouldn't have gone wandering off while someone was breaking into the library," she said. "And if she knows our guest, then it's too bad for them both."

"Diane doesn't know Laney," I said. "She was bluffing, you know that. I think she's on the lowest rung of the Founders' ladder, based on how scared she was when she got caught."

"She can't be," said Estelle. "I mean, they actually turned her into one of them. They don't do that to just anyone, do they?"

"I haven't the faintest idea," Cass said. "If you want to take her to Evangeline, Rory, then I'd suggest you get a move on before I change my mind about feeding her to a book-wraith."

I turned to Aunt Adelaide, who nodded slowly. "Yes... I think it's wise that we should ask the vampires to decide on her fate."

"More than one of us should go," Estelle said. "No, Aunt Candace, not you."

"Spoilsport." Aunt Candace pouted. "I already missed out on the exciting part."

"You won't miss much this time," I told her. "We'll hand Diane over to the vampires, and Evangeline will take care of the rest."

"I'll carry her." Cass flicked her wand, and the comatose vampire's body rose into the air. "Let's move."

"Wait a moment." Since when did Cass willingly venture near the vampires' home? "Hey—Sylvester, cut that out."

The owl, who hovered above the floating prisoner with his beak menacingly close to her ear, gave a disgruntled hoot. "I think you should have let me redecorate her face first."

"No." Aunt Adelaide beckoned to him. "We're going to fix up the library's defences. *How* she got in without being detected..."

Part of me wanted to call Xavier, but there was no telling how the Grim Reaper would react to the news that a partly turned vampire had shown up in town and tried to rob us. The Grim Reaper's rivalry with the vampires was a complex one, and for all I knew, he might even try to Reap Diane's soul before she could complete the transformation.

"I'll help with the defences too," Estelle offered. "Rory... be careful."

"I will." I glanced at Cass, who'd already begun to levitate the vampire's unconscious body across the lobby. "Ah— if Laney comes back—"

"I'll tell her," said Estelle. "Where is she, do you know?"

"She had a vampire lesson tonight, but that was a while ago," I said to Estelle. "She's probably gone for a night-time wander."

"Or to one of her vampire orgies," Cass said in a distasteful tone. "What? It's true. This one might not be one of her human chew toys, but I bet she has a few. She might even share them with the Founders."

"Don't be absurd." My cousin's irrational dislike of Laney aside, Diane clearly wasn't a friend of any of ours. "Laney knows the risk of associating with anyone linked to the Founders. She's also careful not to let Evangeline peek into her thoughts to steal our secrets."

Cass sniffed, seemingly unimpressed. "Whatever."

I hurried to catch up as she levitated the vampire's unconscious body past the desk and out of the front door. The town square was deserted at this hour, and I didn't see a single soul on the high street. *Probably for the best,* I thought as the vampire's head knocked against a lamp post.

"Cass, you could stand to be a bit more careful with her," I said. "We want to question her when she wakes up, remember?"

"Are you certain Evangeline won't tear out her throat the instant she sets eyes on her?" she enquired.

"Well..." *No,* was the honest answer, but I didn't need to encourage Cass to treat our would-be burglar any more roughly than she already had.

When we reached the vampires' home, I knocked on the oak doors, which opened to reveal an unfamiliar vampire. Eerily handsome like all of the undead, he had perfectly symmetrical features, porcelain skin, and pointed teeth that showed when he scowled down at Cass and me.

"I need to talk to Evangeline," I said. "It's urgent."

"She's busy," he said. "Your friend might demand special treatment from our leader, Aurora, but that doesn't mean she'll answer to your every whim."

"This isn't a whim." What was his problem? I'd never even set eyes on him before, but the hostility radiating from his gaze made me want to back away. When he made to close the door, I hastily jammed my foot in the way. "Hang on a moment."

"We have a newly reborn vampire who tried to break into our library," Cass interjected. "If your boss doesn't show up to collect her soon, we're going to use her for target practise."

The vampire eyed the unconscious form of Diane as if noticing her for the first time. "She's not one of ours."

"Why do you think we want to talk to Evangeline?" Cass's belligerent tone drew another scowl from the vampire, but he vanished into the church without another word.

I kept my foot in the doorway to keep the door from closing. "Who's that guy?"

"One of your friend's acquaintants, I'm guessing," said Cass. "You know, it's awfully convenient that she's missing tonight of all nights."

"Her going out at night is no different than us leaving the library during the day." I took a swift step back when Evangeline appeared in the doorway.

"Aurora." Evangeline's gaze travelled across to my cousin. "And Cassandra. What is it this time?"

"She tried to break into the library." I indicated the unconscious vampire hovering behind Cass. "We got her name, Diane, and she said she was there to steal from us—but she passed out cold and doesn't have a pulse. She's undergoing the transformation."

"Is she?" Her teeth gleamed in the moonlight. "Well, I can stop that easily enough."

My heart sank. "If she doesn't wake up, we'll lose our chance to find out who sent her."

"We know who sent her," Cass said. "She came to steal the book of vampire lore. The one *you* gave back to Rory."

"Is that so?" Evangeline's piercing gaze pinned me to the spot. "You chose to bring her to me, Aurora, knowing that?"

"I did." I sensed that I was treading on dangerous ground. "My aunt suggested calling the police given that she tried to break into my family's property, but I thought this ought to be a more appropriate place for her to undergo the transformation."

"Did you now?" She looked into my eyes, and I looked steadily back. I had nothing to hide, after all, including the fact that I'd potentially landed myself in trouble with Edwin by choosing to bring the vampire here without informing him first. "Why exactly should I take on the responsibility for a stray?"

"She won't be a burden, not until she wakes up and we can question her," I said. "Don't you want to know who sent her here? I certainly do."

Evangeline's eyes narrowed a fraction. "We'll see. Joseph, take her to the dungeon."

The dungeon? I didn't know why it surprised me that she had a dungeon in her home, considering, but my heart gave an uneasy flip.

The vampire who'd answered the door, who must be Joseph, flitted out of the church and roughly grabbed Diane. Tension rippled in the air, and he gave a final glare at me and Cass before he carried the unconscious vampire back into the church.

Who's that guy? What does he have against Laney?

"There," said Evangeline. "Now, kindly leave me be."

The door closed. For a brief instant, I debated knocking again and asking if she had any idea why someone had chosen *now* to steal the book, but I didn't need her unfriendly fellow vampire eavesdropping on our business. I'd come back tomorrow instead.

"Friendly," I remarked to Cass. "Any idea what that guy's problem was?"

"Ask your friend." She swept away from the church, and I hastened to keep pace with her.

"I hope Evangeline doesn't change her mind and kill Diane before we find out why she broke into our property," I said as we walked down the deserted high street. Once again, I debated dropping into the cemetery to speak to Xavier, but I'd rather break the news to him while his boss was at arm's length.

"If her curiosity outweighs her bloodlust, she won't," was all Cass said. "It's out of our hands now."

"Yeah, unless whoever sent her here decides to send backup to see where she went."

Cass's eyes narrowed, and she walked on, her hands buried in her pockets. "They'd better not. I knew we shouldn't have taken in that book."

"It's been weeks since Evangeline gave it to us, Cass," I said. "We can hardly throw it out now, can we?"

"No, and I bet that's the reason she willingly gave it up." She quickened her pace. "I bet she wanted to plant the book on us so the vamps wouldn't break into *her* property."

"What—Evangeline?" She might have a point, though it had been the Grim Reaper who'd taken the book off my dad and then given it to the vampires. "She might have known someone would come after it, but so did we. We went into this with our eyes open."

"Some of us did. Others didn't." Cass quickened her pace, her manner indicating the conversation was over.

I didn't begrudge her for being irritated with me for bringing the book into the library, but we wouldn't know the full picture until Diane woke up and told us the truth... assuming Evangeline didn't kill her first.

When we neared the library, I saw Laney waiting on the

doorstep. In front of me, Cass halted and pulled out her wand.

"Hey!" I stepped between her and Laney, alarmed. "There you are, Laney."

"Estelle told me everything," Laney said. "I'm sorry I wasn't here."

Cass stepped around me, lowering her wand. "Honestly. What's the point in having a vampire living in the library if you're never around to help?"

"What about you?" Laney countered. "What did you do to stop the intruder?"

"I'm the one who noticed her sneaking around," Cass said. "She's lucky I didn't stake her in the back, but Rory wanted to find out who sent her. I think you know perfectly well who did, don't you?"

The colour drained from Laney's face, and she backed into the library. I caught the door in my hand before it closed.

"Cass," I said to my cousin, "can you not at least *try* to remember we're all on the same side? Diane's the one you want to interrogate, not Laney. Besides, it was my book she came to steal."

"Then you ought to hand it straight back to the Grim Reaper."

"That... that's not a bad idea," said Aunt Adelaide, from the other side of the door. "Granted, the library holds other valuable titles that would be of interest to the Founders, and there's no guarantee that removing it would prevent us from being targeted again."

"I don't trust the Grim Reaper not to flat-out refuse to take the book back in," I added, joining her inside the library. "Also, I'm not asking him for a favour when I'm not even properly out of debt with Evangeline."

Cass let the door swing shut behind her. "No, and now we've given her another problem to deal with."

"Evangeline took her in, then?" asked Estelle.

"Yes, but Diane can't exactly threaten anyone while she's in a coma," I said. "If I were Evangeline, I'd want to know the truth too. If it *is* the Founders..."

"Weird that they'd send a human though," Laney remarked. "A human on the brink of transforming, true, but not someone smart and sneaky enough to make a decent job of stealing the book. I'd say whoever's running this operation isn't on the tier of Mortimer Vale."

"None of us cares where you rank your sire," said Cass.

Laney flinched at the word. From the awkward silence that ensued, Cass knew she'd gone too far this time, but she didn't apologise. Instead, she walked away, departing in the direction of the stairs.

"Ignore her," I said to Laney. "She was already in a foul mood, and now she's decided we're both to blame for the home invasion."

"Yeah." Her expression remained downcast. "I like to forget *he's* the one who made me like this though."

Mortimer Vale. As her sire, he was connected to her in ways that I didn't understand and frankly didn't want to contemplate. Cass had crossed a line by bringing that up, but while Laney could have easily followed and confronted her, she didn't budge.

"I'll talk to her." Estelle followed Cass's path to the stairs, while Aunt Adelaide made to leave too.

"You did well, Rory," my aunt said. "I think you made the right call by handing her over to Evangeline."

"Yeah... I hope I did." I watched her leave, followed by a reluctant Aunt Candace until Laney and I were alone in the lobby.

Laney raised her gaze to the balconies of the upper floors. "Your cousin was right. I *should* have been here."

"You're allowed to leave the library like the rest of us are," I said. "Nobody else was awake when the intruder came in."

"Except Cass," she said. "Sounds like she was quick on the mark."

"Yeah, and she woke me up first, which was weird," I commented. "I dozed off on the sofa while I was waiting for you to come back."

Guilt flickered across her features. "Sorry. I needed to clear my head after my lesson with Evangeline, so I went for a walk. I didn't know someone was going to break in, let alone one of *them*."

"I don't know why they picked now," I said. "They also didn't send their best. Diane only got as far as she did because she shut Sylvester in an empty classroom."

"Did she?" she asked. "Wow. She was definitely in over her head. Must be a newbie."

"Yeah, but she has to have been in pretty deep if she let one of them bite her." I studied Laney's face, noting that she was careful not to meet my eyes. "I don't know how it works though. How the Founders initiate people, I mean."

"No..." She trailed off noncommittally. "I mean, it's not consistent. Mostly depends on who you know."

A chill raced down my spine. "So you don't know which Founder might have sent her?"

"No, I really don't." Her shoulders hunched and given her obvious discomfort, I opted to drop the subject.

"Cass and I met a vampire who didn't seem to be much of a fan of our family at Evangeline's place," I told her. "Joseph, I think his name was."

"Oh, him." She wrinkled her nose. "He was the newest

vampire recruit before I moved in. I think he got annoyed at me for stealing his glory."

"Really?" If he was new to being a vampire, then he might have known Jeffrey, too... which reminded me that I still hadn't found out who'd turned him.

"Yeah, we stay out of each other's way."

"Wise idea," I said. "Oh yeah, did you manage to get Evangeline to drop any clues about Jeffrey?"

"Nope," she said. "I still have no idea who turned him. I'm not sure *she* knows."

"She doesn't?"

"Yeah, I really think she'd have told us if she did," she said. "With the lengths she's going to avoid answering, she probably doesn't want to admit her ignorance."

"That sounds like her." Still, it was rare for Evangeline to be unaware of anything that occurred among her fellow vampires, let alone a matter as important as the creation of a new vampire.

If she doesn't know, then who does?

10

"You cannot enter the library without answering three riddles." Sylvester's voice drifted upstairs when I walked down from my room the following morning. "One, how long is a broomstick?"

"Sylvester, what are you doing?" I entered the lobby and spied a bewildered Xavier on the other side of the door, which Sylvester had barricaded closed with a disused bookshelf.

"Testing our new security system," the owl said from his perch on top of the shelf. "Everyone who enters the library must prove their worth."

"I'm pretty sure Aunt Adelaide doesn't want you quizzing all our patrons." I beckoned Xavier inside. "Let him in, Sylvester. He's here to see me."

He also must have received the message I'd sent him the previous night given the concerned look in his eyes. I hadn't been able to fit the details of the break-in into a text message, but once the adrenaline had worn off, I'd crashed until dawn.

Sylvester reluctantly moved so that Xavier could walk

around the bookshelf barring the door. He could easily have used his Reaper abilities to bypass the door altogether, but he'd refrained out of politeness, which made the owl's antics even more irritating.

"Really." I beckoned Xavier to follow me into the living quarters since nobody else had come downstairs yet, and I was in dire need of coffee. "I guess you got my message?"

"A *vampire* broke in?"

"Not a vampire, but halfway there." I explained the night's misadventures to him while I grabbed breakfast and poured myself a mug of strong coffee. I had a busy day ahead, including having to break the news to Edwin that I'd handed a criminal over to Evangeline.

"You were lucky." Xavier took a seat opposite me at the kitchen table. "Lucky she was untrained, that is."

"And that Cass woke me up." I sipped my coffee. "Not sure why she did, to be honest. She could have handled the whole thing herself."

"I bet she wanted backup." He glanced over at the clock on the kitchen wall. "I can't stay long. My boss wants me back home for a lesson."

"Don't you already know everything there is to know about how to be a Reaper by now?"

"You'd be surprised," he said. "Actually... well, he's starting to train me on Reaping vampire souls."

I nearly dropped my mug. "Not unwilling ones, I hope."

"No, he's just covering the theory," he clarified. "We won't get to the practical element for a long while."

"I should hope not." A shiver ran down my back. "Interesting timing."

"I thought so, too, but I've been waiting for a while." His steady gaze somewhat soothed my jangling nerves. "Relax,

Rory. It'll be like Reaping any other soul, which is a skill I use in one circumstance only."

"Sure." I let him pull me into a hug, though I couldn't quite banish the thought that the Grim Reaper had chosen to teach him that skill for a reason.

Because he'd expected more vampire deaths to follow.

∿

My meeting with Edwin went about as well as I might have expected. In other words, he looked at me as if I'd brought a live kelpie into the office while I explained how I'd made the decision to hand Diane over to Evangeline last night.

"You gave a person of interest in the murder case over to *her*?" he spluttered.

"There's no proof Diane was linked to Jeffrey's murder." A guilty twinge rose in my chest, all the same. "Also, did you really want someone to transform into a vampire in your prison?"

He shook his head. "It wasn't your call to make."

"It wasn't just my decision." Another twinge of guilt, which I pushed aside. "In fact, Cass wanted to stake Diane there and then, and nobody wanted to keep her overnight in the library. This way is easier."

"You can't expect me to believe your family didn't listen to you at all, Aurora," he said. "You've put me in a very difficult position."

"I'm sorry," I said. "I just didn't want you to have to deal with the possible fallout of keeping her in your prison. There's also a chance the vampires who sent her here might come after her, which would endanger anyone in the area. Anyway, even if they don't, when she becomes a vampire, she'll be Evangeline's responsibility anyway."

He sighed. "I don't want this to end in an argument between us, but I really wish you'd asked me first."

"Our options were limited," I said. "Finding a vampire in the library in the middle of the night isn't exactly something we had a plan for."

"I thought she wasn't a vampire at the time."

"She moved like one of them," I said. "If a human has been drinking a vampire's blood, they gain some of their advantages, for the short-term. I didn't realise she'd been bitten as well before she fell unconscious."

"Who even is she?" he asked. "You said she's not from Ivory Beach?"

"No," I said. "She isn't. She told us her name was Diane, but she fell into a coma before she could answer all our questions."

"She's not one of Evangeline's vampires."

"No, but she *is* a vampire, even if I don't know who turned her." Which reminded me—I hadn't told him my most recent realisation about our murder victim yet. "Also, Laney thinks Evangeline doesn't know who turned Jeffrey into a vampire either."

"The murder victim?" His brows shot up. "If this Diane turns out to be connected to Jeffrey's murder, then it *is* my business. If she had a vampire's abilities, wouldn't she have been able to sneak up on and kill another vampire even before she turned?"

My mouth parted. "Theoretically yes. She struck me as a bit amateur in her methods when she broke into the library, though, and she didn't try to hurt any of us."

"She's obeying someone else, you said." Edwin tutted. "We can't rule out her *or* whoever is giving her orders as potential suspects in Jeffrey's murder, and until then, I cannot let Evangeline be the only person who has access to the prisoner."

I should have seen that one coming. "I'm not denying she might turn out to be the murderer, but she's going to be asleep for a minimum of two days, and even Evangeline won't be able to do anything about it. I don't know that visiting her would do anything other than cause an annoyance."

"Nevertheless," he said, "I cannot help but think you took advantage of my need for your help."

I grimaced. It was fair of him to lose some trust in me after I'd gone behind his back, but I maintained that he and his fellow officers wouldn't have wanted the mentally scarring experience of watching Diane undergo the transformation into one of the living dead. Their cells might be sturdy, but Mortimer Vale had instigated a jailbreak when he'd been imprisoned in Ivory Beach and had ended up being transferred to a more secure prison elsewhere.

"I understand," I said. "If Diane hadn't fallen into a coma, then I might have been able to bring her to you, but I didn't want to risk the safety of you or your fellow officers. When she wakes up, I might be able to convince Evangeline to hand her over if that's what you want."

He studied my face. "I realise that most regular prisons are not designed for vampires, but if she murdered someone... it brings to mind a similar incident some months ago."

My stomach sank. I'd wondered if he might bring up those two vampires' deaths, which had never been officially solved by the police. It was Evangeline who'd held the power to enact punishment on the killer, and she'd chosen to spare Laney's life instead, but that didn't mean I wanted

Edwin to know my best friend had had a brief career as a vampire slayer.

While Diane hadn't known Laney, we'd be in real trouble if any of the Founders had an inkling of her involvement in the murders. Evangeline had taken Laney under her wing to keep her safe from the Founders' possible retaliation, but it would only take one slipup for the truth to reach the wrong person. Laney's recent nocturnal wanders didn't help matters, admittedly, but that was her risk to take.

She wasn't the killer. Not this time... but Diane might have been, and I couldn't rule out her involvement until she woke up.

Edwin gave another sigh. "I've done my level best to reach anyone who Jeffrey was connected to when he was alive, but unless something new comes up, we're left with the two people I already had on the list."

"All right." For both our sakes, I hoped he was telling the truth, but I wouldn't have entirely blamed him if he'd decided to cut me out of the investigation altogether. "I don't think it's the brother."

"Yes, Jeffrey's brother seems to have had little contact with the victim recently," he agreed. "His ex-partner, however, might be worth a second questioning."

"I guess." Eric hadn't given anything away, but it would have been a lot easier if one of us had been able to read *his* mind. Or if the vampires had deigned to help.

Edwin peered at my face. "What are you scheming?"

"Scheming? You make me sound like Aunt Candace," I said. "No, I was just thinking about how it would be easier if we regular people could read minds."

"That would cause more problems than it solved..." He trailed off, looking over my shoulder. "Speak of the devil."

I spun around and saw none other than Aunt Candace

herself sauntering towards the police station. Uh-oh. "I'll be right back."

The automatic doors slid open, and I hurried to waylay my aunt before she could seize on the chance to pounce on Edwin. "What are you doing here?"

"Oh, just going for a walk," she replied cheerily. "I saw you in the police station and thought I'd check and see how you're getting on."

I folded my arms across my chest. "You just happened to walk past, did you?"

"Why, Aurora, I'm insulted that you'd think otherwise."

"You never 'just go for a walk,' Aunt Candace," I informed her. "Also, I'd have thought it'd be too crowded for you out here."

While the weather wasn't as pleasant as the previous day, tourists and locals alike gathered on the seafront, thronging the pier and the various stalls and rides. Estelle must be among them, though she didn't seem to have noticed our aunt's unwanted approach.

Aunt Candace sniffed. "I'm insulted, Rory. Thoroughly wounded."

"So you don't want to know what Edwin and I talked about?"

Her attention refocused on me. "Well, if you're offering..."

"I have nothing whatsoever to share except that he's annoyed with me for handing a murder suspect over to Evangeline."

"Oh, I didn't know she was a suspect," she said. "Interesting."

"She's not—yet," I clarified. "I don't think Diane killed Jeffrey, personally, but she's out for the count for a couple of days, which kind of puts us at a standstill. Sorry to disappoint you."

"I shall see what I can uncover." She turned back towards the pier with a determined stride.

"Hey, I never said you had to do any investigating yourself," I said. "If anything, there are more investigators than actual suspects."

Unless you counted Diane as a suspect... and Laney.

Aunt Candace strode onwards to the row of stalls running parallel to the beach, where I caught sight of Estelle near the stall with the cuddly dragons.

"Hey, Rory." Estelle waved me over. "Hey, Aunt Candace. I'm surprised to see you out here."

"No trouble today?" I asked in a low voice when I reached her side. "That shifter hasn't come back?"

"No, but I'm on the lookout," she said. "I won't let him steal anything else."

"Stealing, you say?" asked Aunt Candace. "Who was stealing?"

"You saw that shifter who tried to win all those cuddly dragons the other day, didn't you?" I indicated the stall, which was once again staffed by the rat shifter, who seemed none the worse for wear after the shifter's destructive temper tantrum.

"Those are delightful," she said. "I think I'll try to win one again myself."

Aunt Candace sauntered towards the stall and addressed the startled rat shifter. "Yes, I'd like another try, please."

"Should I rescue him?" I whispered to Estelle.

"Let her try," said Estelle. "It'll keep her amused."

"Or keep her from pestering Edwin," I added. "He's not thrilled with me either. I think I shook his trust in me by handing Diane over to Evangeline."

She pursed her lips. "I doubt he'd want to watch a vampire transforming in his jail, but I guess going behind his back wouldn't have gone down well."

"Pretty much," I said. "And now we're down to zero suspects. Unless one of us finds evidence to implicate either one of Jeffrey's contacts."

Or I asked Laney to read their minds, but that would involve going behind Edwin's back again.

Aunt Candace yelled aloud in celebration, and the bemused rat shifter handed her a giant cuddly dragon.

"It's like distracting a toddler," I said to Estelle. "I should get her back to the library before she gets any more wild ideas."

"Fair point," said Estelle. "I'm sorry Edwin wasn't more understanding. Maybe you'll have more luck with the vampires."

"Considering our only suspect is unconscious, I'm not sure on that one." I eyed Aunt Candace, who'd cradled the dragon in her arms and murmured to it as if it was her familiar. "Aunt Candace, come on. Let's head back to the library."

Aunt Candace rolled her eyes at me. "Really, that isn't necessary. I'll behave myself."

"I was going back there already," I said. "It's not fair of you to leave Aunt Adelaide to do all the work on the library's defences."

"Speak for yourself." She stepped out of the way of a pack of teenagers laden with giant ice creams, who were chattering at the top of their voices. "I suppose it *is* rather noisy."

She let me steer her away from the crowds and down the street alongside the clock tower. Even the town square was busier than usual, and the usual everyday shoppers mingled with the tourists crowding Zee's bakery and the other shops. Summer was a great time for local businesses, but the trouble with so many strangers being in town was that I had no chance of knowing if any of the normal-looking witches and wizards secretly spent their free time hanging out with the Founders.

As we neared the library, someone stepped into view, drawing me to a surprised halt. Jeffrey's ex-boyfriend, Eric. What was he doing here?

11

I approached Eric, surprised to see him outside the library. Was Sylvester quizzing our patrons and refusing to let them in again?

"Hey," I said to Eric. "If you want to check out a book, then you can come in."

"It's you I wanted to talk to."

"Me?" I was conscious of Aunt Candace hovering behind me, still chattering to her cuddly dragon. "Okay, we'll go inside. Come on, Aunt Candace."

My aunt looked up at me and then at Eric. "Who's this?"

"No one," Eric said quickly. "I'm no one."

"Nobody is no one," said Aunt Candace. "Unless that's your name? How intriguing."

The library door opened, sparing him from having to answer, and Aunt Adelaide poked her head out. "Candace, please come in here and give me a hand with this."

At a guess, she must have heard us talking and correctly assumed Aunt Candace was in one of her annoying moods.

Aunt Candace sighed theatrically. "Fine, I suppose we can help, right, Brutus?"

She'd already named her dragon? "You know he's not real, right?" Not that that was the prevailing issue here.

Aunt Candace covered the dragon's ears. "Don't say that, you'll hurt his feelings."

Honestly.

When Aunt Adelaide had shepherded her sister into the library, I turned to Eric. "Sorry about that. We can talk in there."

Eric reluctantly followed me in, staring around at the lobby as if concerned the library might try to eat him alive. Given Sylvester's new security measures, that thought might not be that far off the mark. I led him towards the Reading Corner, hoping Aunt Candace was too busy dealing with whatever task her sister had dumped on her head to eavesdrop on us.

"What did you want to talk to me about?" I asked Eric when we reached the cosy area at the back of the lobby. "Ah—have you seen the police since the last time?"

"The police? No."

Hmm. Maybe I should have insisted he talk to Edwin instead of me, but I didn't need to frighten him off. His manner reminded me of a cornered animal on the brink of making a bolt for it, though part of me wondered if I ought to wake Laney so her vampire senses would be able to catch him out if he lied.

"Look," said Eric. "Maybe this isn't a good idea. I don't know why I came here, really, but I can't talk to anyone else."

"Is it about Jeffrey?" I asked. "It is, right?"

"I just wanted to know what happened to him," he mumbled. "I can't exactly go and pester the vampires, and if I go back to the police, they might get suspicious. I don't *know* who killed him. Honestly."

He certainly sounded sincere, but how could I be sure? "Were you telling the truth when you said that you didn't know Jeffrey had any links with the vampires before he turned? Because if you weren't, then I can't help you until you're completely honest with me."

He took in a ragged breath. Then he startled and gasped, "Vampire!"

I whirled around, and Laney sheepishly emerged from behind a shelf, her steps as stealthy and graceful as ever. How long had she been standing there? "Laney?"

Eric backed away. "I didn't know you had one of them living here. This was a mistake."

I caught Laney's eye, confused as to why she was up at this hour. I'd debated waking her so she could peer into Eric's thoughts, but I hadn't expected her to rouse herself of her own accord when she couldn't possibly have known he was here.

"Don't leave on my account," Laney said to him, her tone surprisingly hostile. "Care to explain why I can't read your mind?"

Eric moved to flee, but Laney blocked his path, seizing his arm with the casual strength of a vampire.

"Whoa." I looked between them, alarmed. "Laney, you can't read his mind? Really?"

"Tell me why," she told him. "Go on."

He groaned. "Please let me go. I don't know anything."

"You clearly know the vampires," said Laney.

He shook his head frantically. "No, except Jeffrey, and like I said, he cut off all contact with me when he turned."

"Why can't she read your mind, then?" I asked. "There's no innocent reason for that to be possible."

In fact, if he'd somehow protected himself against mind control, he could only have got the means of doing so from a vampire himself. His expression showed confusion and fear, followed by recognition. Slowly, he reached a shaking hand into the collar of his shirt, pulling out a glowing round stone attached to a pendant he wore around his neck.

"It... it might be this," he mumbled. "Jeff gave it to me himself. He said it would protect me from them."

"Did he now?" Laney tilted her head without releasing his other arm. "I've only ever seen people who attend the Founders' parties wearing those."

His mouth tightened. "Jeff said he wanted me to have this, that it would keep me safe from the other—vampires. I don't know anything more, I swear."

"Did he have a good reason to believe you'd be a target?" asked Laney. "That pendant might be able to stop another vampire from reading your mind, but it won't do a thing to prevent them from ripping out your throat."

He squeezed his eyes shut. "I swear I don't know anything. He only wanted to protect me, nothing more."

"Then would you mind handing that thing over to us?" I watched Laney with concern. I hadn't seen her in full-on vampire mode for a while, and the result was scarier than I'd have liked to admit. "You must have some idea why Jeffrey thought you might be a target."

"He didn't say." His trembling fingers reached for the pendant. "Is that all? If I give you the pendant, you'll let me go?"

"Not until you've answered a couple of questions *without* that thing around your neck," Laney said. "If you're lying, then I'll know."

I held out a hand for the pendant. "Laney won't hurt you, but I can't say the same of the people who made that, if it's who I think it is."

The Founders had given Laney a potion that temporarily made her immune to mind reading, but they must have upgraded their efforts if they were making magical pendants with the same effect. And if Jeffrey had once been the pendant's owner, then he must have been in deep. Why, then, had he given it away, and might that have led to his death?

With trembling fingers, Eric looped the pendant over his head and dropped it into my outstretched hand. Laney released him, and he stumbled back a step, rubbing his arm. "Okay. You can read my mind now, right? You should see that I'm telling the truth."

Laney shook her head. "No. It'll take a bit for the effects to fade. You might need to be farther away from that pendant too."

"Should I shut it in a room somewhere?" I turned the gleaming stone over in my hands. "Would that help?"

"Can't hurt." She eyed Eric. "If you don't move, I won't grab you again. Deal?"

That would have to do. I crossed the lobby to the Reading Corner, found the first empty classroom available, and tossed the pendant inside. I then shut the door and cast a locking charm, hoping it'd be enough to dissuade anyone from wandering in.

When I returned to Eric and Laney, neither of them had moved. Good. I didn't entirely trust Eric's motives, but I didn't relish the idea of watching Laney unleash her vampiric fury on him either.

"Any better?" I asked her. "Can you read his thoughts?"

Her brow screwed up. "Yeah... it's coming back. Gradually."

"Who made that pendant?" I directed the question at Eric.

He shook his head. "I don't know. Like I said, Jeff gave it to me, and—you know I'm telling the truth now."

"Yeah, I guess you are." Laney gave him a considering look. "That means you really didn't know Jeffrey was hanging out with vampires in his spare time?"

"Not until he came back as one of them." He lowered his gaze, his shoulders hunched. "When it was too late."

"Not quite." Laney took a step closer to him with the languid grace of a vampire about to pounce. "You aren't telling me everything."

He backed away from her, fetching up against a bookshelf. "No. I told you everything, I swear."

Laney tilted her head to one side. "Why did you think you could hide your thoughts from a vampire?"

His face crumpled. "I don't know anything of value. I swear. Please."

"You *did* know he was spending his free time outside of Ivory Beach."

"I can't begrudge him for having a social life, especially while he was out of work," he said defensively. "He was always more into the party scene than I was, and there's not much of that around here."

"Where?" I asked. "Do you know specifics?"

Eric shook his head. "I *wish* I knew more, but he wouldn't tell me anything about where he went or who he met with. He wanted to keep me safe. He wouldn't have given me the pendant otherwise."

"You know I can't let you have it back though," I said. "Also, you should speak to the police again. Edwin won't have you listed as a suspect now that you've had a vampire read your thoughts, and you might need the police's protection if they *do* come looking for you. It's up to you though."

I couldn't think why the Founders would target a regular

person, but there was no telling what Jeffrey had been into before his death. Not when he hadn't even told the guy he'd been dating. Admittedly, Edwin wasn't in the best of moods with me, and for a lot of people, the word of a vampire wasn't exactly hard evidence. Nobody on the police force could read minds, after all.

As for Eric himself, he'd be entirely vulnerable if the Founders came searching. Even the police might not be able to help him. Evangeline might, but would she offer help to a human? Doubtful.

"I don't know." Eric took a few steps back, one eye on Laney as if afraid she might grab his arm again. "If they come for me, then it'll be obvious I don't know anything."

"That's your risk to take," said Laney. "Go on, hop to it, and stop looking at me as if I'm going to bite you. You're not my type."

"Laney." I elbowed her in the ribs, while Eric gave us one last frightened look and then fled across the lobby. "You went a bit far there. Were you channelling Cass?"

"Sorry." She yawned. "I get cranky when I wake up during the day."

"Why *were* you awake?"

She shrugged one shoulder. "Even vampires get insomnia."

True enough. I'd had a disturbed rest myself the previous night, thanks to the break-in, but I didn't know if that was on her mind or something else. Nor did I know how to ask without alluding to subjects she didn't want to discuss.

Laney caught me studying her face. "I'm fine, Rory. It's just been a weird week. I didn't expect *them* to resurface out of nowhere, let alone find out they're expanding their recruitment efforts."

"Expanding their efforts?" I echoed. "How do you mean?"

"Diane and Jeffrey both knew about the paranormal world before they turned into vampires—well, the latter did," she said. "They're not just recruiting normals anymore."

"Good point." Not only that, but they'd recruited someone from Ivory Beach—and from underneath Evangeline's nose. Yes, he seemed to have spurned them given that he'd gone to live in Evangeline's home and had even handed over the pendant they'd gifted him to his ex-boyfriend instead of keeping it for himself... but what if he wasn't the only person they'd targeted?

Their leader might be in jail, but Mortimer Vale had been only one of the vampires who ran the Founders. I'd never met the others. Had Laney though?

"I never met him before now," Laney said. "In case it wasn't obvious. In fact, I've never met another vampire in Ivory Beach who I recognised from one of *their* gatherings."

"Might be a good thing you haven't." Yet the Founders were undeniably stepping up their game. "I think I need to talk to Evangeline later when she's awake. She needs to see that pendant."

Except if I did, I'd be going behind Edwin's back for the second time in two days. Evangeline was unlikely to let anyone other than herself keep the pendant, but to Edwin, it might count as evidence.

"I don't know if she'd be able to figure out where it came from." Laney followed me to the room in which I'd left the pendant and watched me undo the unlocking charm on the door. "Honestly, you're better off keeping it for yourself."

"You can't be serious." The idea of rendering Evangeline permanently unable to break into my mind wasn't unappealing, but if she figured out where I'd got the pendant, she'd conclude that I was in league with her enemies and act accordingly.

"No, you're right, that's a bad idea." She stood back while I opened the door—and stared into an empty classroom.

The pendant had gone.

"Rory?" Laney peered through the door behind me. "Is the pendant in there?"

"Apparently not." I paced into the room, looking under the classroom tables, but found nothing. "Maybe the library ate it, like Cass threatened to do to that vampire."

She blinked at me. "Is that a thing?"

"Not to my knowledge." The library was teeming with secrets, but why would it have taken away a tool as useful as the pendant? Unless Sylvester had wanted to avoid me giving it to Evangeline? I'd seen no signs of the owl since his unpleasant encounter with Diane the previous night, but for all I knew, he'd rigged the library's magic to snatch up anything that looked suspicious.

"Might be for the best," said Laney. "That way you won't have to mediate another argument between Edwin and Evangeline."

"It's hardly going to help the situation," I said. "Edwin was so irked at me for going to Evangeline before I spoke to him that he hinted that he regretted asking me to help at all."

"Ouch," she said. "Was it ever going to end any other way though? He doesn't want a visit from the Founders himself, I'm sure."

"No, but Evangeline isn't going to be happy either." Not if I admitted I'd somehow lost a valuable piece of evidence inside my own home. "Do you think I should mention Eric's visit? He *is* innocent, right? You didn't see anything suspect when you read his thoughts?"

"Nope," she said. "He's innocent of everything except dating someone who was seeing the Founders in his free time but didn't tell him. Oh, and taking that pendant without asking what it did."

I closed the classroom door then opened it again. "Where *is* the pendant? It can't be nowhere."

It must be in the library at the very least, which meant I'd be able to find it using the Book of Questions. In theory, depending on whether Sylvester was in an accommodating mood, and on whether I wanted to risk using up my one daily question when I might need another one later. Not that I'd felt the need to use the Book for a while. Its knowledge concerned the library and nothing more, and the murder wasn't remotely connected to anything the library's resources had the power to solve.

Instead, I searched the other classrooms lining the back wall behind the Reading Corner. Laney kept yawning, so I ordered her to go back to bed. She compensated by planting herself in a hammock and promptly fell asleep. I was glad that Estelle wasn't running one of her poetry workshops today because Laney was so unnervingly still when she was sleeping that I had to remind myself that vampires didn't need to breathe.

After I'd confirmed the pendant wasn't in any of the classrooms, I went to search the stacks and spotted a harried-looking Aunt Adelaide hurrying towards the stairs.

"Hey, Rory," she said. "Can you take over from me on the desk? I'm afraid we have a bit of a situation upstairs."

"What kind of situation?"

"The book-wyrms are back."

"They are?" Of all the timing. "I can, but—did you hear Laney and me talking to that guy in the Reading Corner?"

"Laney's up?"

"Yes, but she's asleep over there." I pointed over my shoulder. "Jeffrey's ex-boyfriend came back to plead with us to solve the murder, and he had this pendant the Founders gave him—"

An alarming crash came from upstairs, followed by a howl of pain that sounded distinctly like Aunt Candace.

Aunt Adelaide winced. "If I were you, I'd have sent him to Edwin instead."

"I advised him to go to the police after he left the library, but I'm not sure he will." I looked uncertainly up at the stairs, where Aunt Candace's legs dangled through a gap between the second and third floors. "Is Sylvester playing tricks again?"

"The book-wyrms have discovered a taste for more than just books," Aunt Adelaide said grimly. "Little devils. I'm trying to convince Cass to help me clear them out, but I'm not having much luck."

"I'll help."

For now, it seemed that finding the pendant would have to wait.

12

Thanks to the book-wyrm infestation, I had to put my plans to visit Evangeline on hold, though considering she slept during the day and the pendant had yet to show up, it was probably for the best. The real miracle was how Laney managed to sleep through the whole thing, including the racket that ensued when several shelves collapsed on the third floor and released a number of wild encyclopaedias.

It took my aunts and me nearly an hour to recapture them, thanks to Cass's unwillingness to help. While running up and downstairs, each of us fell so frequently through the gaps that the infesting insects had chewed in the stairs that Aunt Adelaide lost her patience and performed a spell that somehow created a three-story chute that led from the balconies down to the ground floor so we could slide down instead. Not that it was a perfect method.

"Gangway!" crowed Aunt Candace, zooming down the slide with her hair streaming wildly behind her and landing in a pile of beanbags with a thump. Even *that* didn't wake Laney, which was kind of impressive.

"That's enough." Aunt Adelaide marched over to her. "I think we've dealt with all the wyrms, unless there are more hiding under the shelves."

"How did it get this bad?" I asked. "Did Cass smuggle a couple of them out of the first batch after all?"

"There's a distinct possibility that she did."

Oh boy. That would explain why Cass was avoiding everyone, though at least it would delay the inevitable moment when I had to tell her about Eric's visit to the library and the confirmation that Jeffrey had indeed been meeting with the Founders before his death. As for *why* he'd died, though, I was as much in the dark as ever.

We didn't clear out all the wyrms until early evening when things calmed down enough that I finally had a spare moment to go looking for the missing pendant. To Aunt Candace's eternal dismay, Aunt Adelaide had dismantled the chute, so I took the opportunity to search the Reading Corner while I put all the cushions and beanbags back where they'd come from.

"The wyrms aren't hiding in here, are they?" Estelle walked over, having returned from the carnival, and watched me search under cushions and beanbags.

"Nope, they're mostly upstairs—or they were before Sylvester ate them."

As it turned out, no magical means of extermination worked quite as well as setting the owl loose on the infestation.

"Lovely." Estelle did a double take when she saw Laney sleeping in the hammock. "What's she doing downstairs?"

"Eric paid us a visit," I told her.

"Who?" She blinked. "Wait, wasn't he one of the suspects?"

"Jeffrey's ex." I glanced at Laney, who'd begun to stir.

"Laney couldn't read his thoughts, and it turned out he was wearing a pendant that Jeffrey gave him before he died."

"Really?" Her eyes rounded. "Did Jeffrey get it from *them*?"

"From the Founders, yeah." Laney yawned, sitting upright. "How long was I out?"

"Long enough to miss all the action," I replied. "Wyrms, not vampires, don't worry."

"Ugh." She pushed herself upright. "I'd rather have the vampires. Did you find the pendant?"

"Unfortunately not." To Estelle, I added, "I stashed the pendant in an empty room so we could properly question Eric, and it vanished while my back was turned. The room was locked, so unless a book-wyrm ate it, I've no idea where it went."

"Weird," she commented. "Did you ask Sylvester?"

"No. I'll see if he's finished snacking." I tilted my head back and spied the owl sleeping off his feast on top of the first-floor balcony. "Sylvester?"

"Hmmm." The owl made an indistinct noise but otherwise didn't stir.

"Sylvester?" I asked, louder. "I have a question."

He didn't open his eyes. "You know who to ask."

"The Forbidden Room. Yes, I know, but I thought it'd be quicker this way. Have you seen a pendant?"

"I may have eaten one."

"Sylvester!"

"What?" His eyes opened in annoyance. "What is so important that it's worth interrupting my sleep?"

"A pendant that stops a vampire's mind-reading power," I said. "I put it down in an empty classroom, and it vanished."

"Did you now?" He yawned. "Well, you already elected

to let your friend rummage around in your thoughts, so you don't really need it, do you?"

"That's not the point, Sylvester." I shook my head at him. "The pendant is possible evidence in a murder case. That's why I need it back."

"Sounds like it was careless of you to lose it." He closed his eyes and gave a loud, false snore.

I turned back to Laney and Estelle. "I'm going to have to tell Evangeline. Even without the pendant itself, she needs to know the Founders are recruiting people from Ivory Beach."

"I think she already knows," said Laney. "Not much escapes her."

"Then why doesn't she know who turned Jeffrey?" Unless she did, and she'd opted not to tell us. "Or Diane? She's not local, but the Founders sent her here, and Evangeline can't possibly believe it's an isolated incident."

Aunt Adelaide came ambling over to us. "Rory, were you trying to ask Sylvester something? I have more wyrms to bribe him with, if he can possibly eat another bite."

"You know I told you about that pendant I lost earlier?" I went over my encounter with Eric again since we'd been chasing runaway books around when I'd tried to explain it earlier, and I didn't really blame her for not taking in a word.

"You weren't thinking of telling Evangeline?" she queried. "Or handing the pendant over? It seems like a valuable artefact to have on hand."

"I don't know anyone else who might be able to figure out who it originally belonged to," I admitted. "Except Diane, but we have another day or two before we'll be able to get any sense out of her."

Estelle cleared her throat. "Laney, do you remember any

of the other vampires who held influence among the Founders back when they tried to recruit you?"

Laney's moment of hesitation made my blood chill. "You do?"

She wasn't going to their gatherings again, was she? I'd come to accept her nocturnal wanderings, but I'd never for a minute believed that she'd do anything that might put my family in harm's way.

"I..." She gave an uneasy pause. "This is going to sound terrible, but I've kind of been spying on them."

The breath left my lungs. "*Laney*. You know how risky it is. If they saw you—"

"They didn't," she said. "I only went back to a couple of the places they held gatherings so I could peer in through the windows from the outside. Honestly, I didn't see much. It'd have been easier to get useful information if I'd gone inside."

"No way," I said. "They'd have your head. You killed two of them, remember?"

"I know." Her hands fisted at her sides. "I know, but I wanted to do *something,* and it's not hard for me to cover long distances at night and be back in town by morning. Anyway, there's one local manor house that they've been holding frequent gatherings at, so I assume that's where Diane came from."

"You can't walk back into their lair, Laney."

"*You* certainly can't," she said. "If the Founders are familiar with Ivory Beach, and if they knew Mortimer Vale, they'll know who you are the instant they see into your mind. No matter how careful you are, it'll only take one slipup for them to realise you got one of their ringleaders jailed and that you have something they desire inside the library."

"They already know, Laney." After all, they'd sent Diane to steal the book. "I need to tell Evangeline that the Founders gave Jeffrey the pendant, at the very least, and hope that she forgives us for losing the evidence."

"What about Edwin?" asked Aunt Adelaide. "He wasn't best pleased with you earlier, I take it?"

"Nope, and this will only make it worse," I said. "Unless someone else wants to tell him?"

"I can," Estelle interjected. "I was actually going to head back to the carnival this evening since it's going so well, but I thought I'd drop back here first."

"If you're sure," I said. "You might have to talk him out of marching over to see Evangeline himself. He implied he wants to talk to Diane."

"Nah, he's too sensible to take the risk," she said.

"Tell you what, take Jet with you," I said. "He can keep an eye out for trouble."

"Isn't trouble more likely to come from the vampires?"

I glanced at Laney. "How mad do you think she'll be that I lost the pendant?"

"Less angry than she was that Diane sneaked into town under her nose," Laney said. "I'll come with you."

With no time to lose, Laney and I left the library for the vampires' home. While it was early evening, the sun had yet to sink in the sky, and the noise from the seafront was as upbeat as ever. I didn't blame Estelle for wanting to spend as much time as possible out there.

Laney didn't say much as we walked, while I pondered on what she remembered of her early encounters with the vampires back when she'd been human. I'd thought she'd told me everything, but her recent revelation reminded me that I'd never found out the actual locations of the Founders' gatherings.

When we reached the vampires' home, I knocked on the door to the church. This time, Evangeline herself answered.

"Back already, Aurora?" she asked. "I do hope you have an actual update this time."

"I do... well, I don't have any new suspects, just more clues I can't make sense of." I glanced at Laney. "I spoke to the guy who was dating Jeffrey again, and he admitted that... that Jeffrey gave him a pendant to stop vampires from reading his mind. To protect him, he said."

"A pendant?" Her brow arched. "Where is it now?"

"It's gone. I don't know where it is." Not a lie. I knew my vagueness would annoy her, but I didn't need her tearing up the library in search of it, and if the library itself had hidden the pendant from sight, then it would likely only show itself to a family member.

She bared her teeth. "Really, now. Either you're lying to me, or you're admitting that you obtained and then *lost* a valuable piece of evidence."

"I intend to find it again, but I wanted you to know what Eric told us. He said that Jeffrey was spending his free time with the vampires before he turned into one—"

"I could have inferred as much myself from his fate," she said. "Do you have any *new* information?"

"I thought it was news that the Founders gave him that pendant." I gave another surreptitious sideways glance at Laney. "It's stronger than the potion they used to give people to block mind reading, so I assume Jeffrey was deep in their inner circle."

"A logical assumption, but I would like to talk to this Eric myself."

"Ah—I think he's talking to the police at the moment." I hoped he was, anyway. "He's scared they'll come back. The Founders."

"He never saw them himself though," Laney added. "Jeffrey gave him the pendant without telling him it would stop them from reading his thoughts. He doesn't know anything."

Evangeline's expression remained unconvinced. "Until I see the pendant for myself, it's impossible for me to verify its source."

"Who else could have given it to him?" Another possibility hit me. "Hang on—did Diane have one of those pendants too?"

Laney shifted. "That's a good question. Did she?"

No answer came from Evangeline, whose lips pursed.

"Didn't you search her before you took her in?" Admittedly, Diane had been in a coma at the time, so nobody would have had any reason to try reading her mind or to search her for weapons. "Can we see her?"

Irritation tugged at Evangeline's otherwise flawless face. "I'd advise you not to vex me, Aurora. The prisoner is lucky I didn't simply kill her on sight."

"I know, but I thought you wanted to keep her alive to question her later." This was going downhill fast. "She's likely not a major player, but the Founders sent her here, and I'm pretty sure the same people turned Jeffrey into a vampire too. Did you ask him anything about his past when you took him in?"

She glowered at me in answer, her teeth on display once again. I'd probably crossed a line by asking impertinent questions, but it seemed uncharacteristic of her to take in strays. She'd taken in Laney, true, but Mortimer Vale was in prison and therefore no threat to Evangeline.

If, like Laney had suggested, Evangeline didn't *know* who'd turned Jeffrey... then it opened a new avenue of questions. And if I wanted to find out who was behind his murder and the recent incursion into our library, then I'd need to know all the details—even the ones the vampires' leader didn't want me to know.

"You understand nothing, Aurora," she said softly. "The world is changing. At one time it was usual for a vampire to be tied to their sire, but not anymore."

Good job, considering who'd turned Laney into a vampire. Mortimer Vale occupied enough space in my nightmares as it was without adding the horrifying idea of him exerting control over Laney's fate. But Evangeline's manner suggested she'd caught a glimpse of my curious thoughts and didn't appreciate them in the least.

"You're right, I don't know everything about the vampires," I said in an attempt to placate her. "But if it's possible to find out who turned Jeffrey, then that information should lead straight to the person responsible for his death."

"There's no way to track the sire of a dead vampire," she said.

"Then what about a living one? Like Diane?" We were back to the prisoner again. "Can't you check to see if she's carrying one of those pendants on her? You don't have to invite us in."

Evangeline gave me a hard stare. "If it stops you from hassling me with inane questions..."

She vanished midsentence, while Laney stirred at my side. "I'm not sure she was being entirely honest."

"What makes you say that?"

"I don't know." She rubbed her forehead. "She's usually reluctant to answer questions, but this time felt different. I can't explain why."

Evangeline reappeared before I could make sense of the idea that Laney seemed to have any level of sensitivity to the leading vampire's moods. "No, she does not have a pendant of any sort."

"Then can I—?" I flinched back when she bared her fangs at me. "Okay, never mind."

"Why not?" Laney stepped in. "Why don't you want Rory to see her? It won't do any harm."

"You," said Evangeline, "ought to know better than to cross any more lines with me."

Laney's jaw tensed. "Where is she? Diane?"

"I don't appreciate that tone of yours." Evangeline took a step closer, her eyes narrowing. "Perhaps I've been too lenient with you."

"Wait a moment," I said hastily. "I don't know what's happening here, but aren't the Founders the real concern? They might be plotting their next attempt to infiltrate Ivory Beach while we argue among ourselves."

Evangeline swivelled towards me. "That isn't news to me, Aurora. As for you, Elaine, if you want to feign ignorance, then that's your prerogative."

Laney blanched at Evangeline's use of her full name. "Ignorance? Of what?"

"Come and look for yourself."

Despite her ominous words, Laney obeyed. I had zero clue if her invitation had included me, but I wasn't about to let her take my best friend out of my sight, so I tailed them both into the church.

At once, my attention snapped over to a low wooden table, on which lay the body of Diane, the prisoner.

A stake protruded from her chest. She was dead—permanently this time.

I stared in horror. "Who did that? I thought your people didn't use stakes against each other."

Except, perhaps, for the killer... but how could they have broken into Evangeline's home? How was it possible?

Evangeline spoke without turning around. "Some of us, it seems, are less inclined to obey the rules than others."

"You think *I* did that?" Laney choked in disbelief. "I wanted her to stay alive to be questioned too."

"You've been keeping secrets from me. I know it." Evangeline's gaze cut to me, and my heart sank. Laney had been working hard to keep the details of my dad's journal from reaching Evangeline, but I hadn't realised she'd been quite that effective at shutting the vampire's leader out. Hadn't known it was possible, in fact.

"Read my mind," Laney said to her. "You'll know I'm telling the truth when I say I didn't kill her."

Evangeline shook her head. "That doesn't erase the secrets you've kept. I've been too lenient on you."

I could hardly breathe. "Don't hurt her on my account. This is my fault—"

"No, it isn't," she said. "It's not simply your own small-minded secrets she's kept hidden, isn't that right, Elaine? You've been quite busy in your free time recently. Am I right?"

No. She knows Laney has been visiting the Founders to spy on them.

Laney lowered her head. "I'll tell you anything you want to know."

"We shall see," said Evangeline. "I conveniently have an empty cell in my dungeon for you to wait in while you think on your transgressions."

My heart leapt into my throat. "No. You can't imprison Laney—not when someone already broke into your jail and killed Diane."

"Elaine knew the risks when I took her in." Her expression was unforgiving. "I have no sympathy."

I shouldn't have expected any sympathy, but Laney's meek submission tugged at my heart. "It's more my fault than hers. I'm the one who told her to hide her thoughts."

"You didn't have any influence over her," she said. "She made the choice herself. Elaine, come with me."

"You can't—"

"There's nothing I cannot do, Aurora, and if you want to avoid joining her in the dungeon, then I suggest you leave. Unless you wish to bargain with me, but there's nothing short of access to your father's journal that might be worth offering in trade."

"That's not—"

I've been a fool. I'd felt so safe in assuming Evangeline wasn't working for the Founders that I'd forgotten just how dangerous she was... and I'd forgotten that despite all the times she'd helped me, she still coveted the journal.

"Well?" she said. "If you're declining my offer, then I suggest you leave."

"I don't understand why you want the journal so badly." The words burst out of me before I could stop them. "If it's because you want whatever information's inside it, then wouldn't the Founders be able to steal that knowledge from your thoughts anyway, given the chance?"

"None but the strongest vampire can access my thoughts, Aurora."

Then why had Laney been able to keep her thoughts hidden from her?

Wait. A sudden horrible thought hit me, and the predatory gleam in Evangeline's eyes suggested she'd seen it too. At once, instinct kicked in and drove me to run, fleeing the church. I didn't stop to breathe until I was sure I'd left her far behind me.

Along with Laney.

Laney. I'd left her to Evangeline's mercy, but she was stronger than I'd ever believed. Strong enough to hide her thoughts from her master... and there was only one reason that might be possible.

Mortimer Vale was stronger than Evangeline, and he was the one who'd turned Laney.

13

When I returned to the library, trying in vain to hold back tears, the person I least wanted to see was Cass. Naturally, as luck would have it, she was the only member of my family in the lobby when I walked in.

"What's up with you?" she asked. "Did your friend ditch you?"

"Evangeline locked Laney in the dungeon," I said thickly, wiping my eyes on my sleeve. "For keeping secrets from her. She did it to protect us, including you, so I don't need to hear any smug comments, thanks."

She blinked. "Evangeline locked her up? What do you mean by secrets?"

"The journal's contents, among other things. That isn't important." I drew in a breath. "Diane is dead. Someone got into the dungeon and staked her in the heart, and Evangeline thinks it was Laney."

"Wasn't it?" Cass queried. "I can't say I'm surprised that someone bumped off our intruder. Honestly, I should have staked her myself and saved her the bother."

"Cass." Why had I even expected any level of understanding from her? "Laney didn't do it, but Evangeline has locked her in the dungeon while there might be a killer on the loose in the vampires' home."

"What did your friend expect when she kept secrets from her vampire boss?" Cass asked. "If she went behind Evangeline's back, it's no surprise. I doubt the killer's looking for her, anyway. They went for Diane because she was working with the enemy."

With the Founders. But if word got out that Laney had been spying on them in her free time, would they strike against her too?

"Mortimer Vale turned her against her will, Cass," I said, my voice brittle. "She was left with the choice to trust Evangeline or die, and you can't say you wouldn't have tried to hide your thoughts from her if you had to spend every waking moment in her company either."

"Your dad's journal isn't *that* important."

"Sure, it's not like anyone's died for it or anything," I retaliated. "Never mind the journal. Where's your mum?"

"I thought you dragged her to see Evangeline too."

"I didn't." I scanned the lobby, but I didn't see any signs of the others, even Sylvester. "Estelle went to talk to the police, and she took Jet with her."

"Why on earth did she go to the police?"

"To tell Edwin that Jeffrey's ex visited the library. Didn't you know?"

"What?" She narrowed her eyes. "Nobody told *me* that."

"Probably because you were hiding up on the third floor while the rest of us cleared out the day's wyrm infestation." I folded my arms across my chest. "I don't suppose you had anything to do with that?"

"Believe it or not, I didn't," she said. "I gave the wyrms I found up on the third floor to Sylvester. Tell me what I missed, then."

"Eric—Jeffrey's ex-boyfriend—admitted that Jeffrey gave him a pendant to prevent vampires from reading his mind, shortly before he was murdered," I said. "I went to tell Evangeline, and that's when we found out our prisoner died too. Look, I have to find your mum. I'm going—"

"No you don't." Sylvester popped up from behind the desk, apparently having woken from his wyrm-induced nap. "You're not to leave the library, either of you."

"Were you listening to any of that?" I asked. "Diane was staked to death in Evangeline's dungeon, and the vampires have arrested Laney in her place. Where *is* Aunt Adelaide?"

"She decided to accompany her eldest daughter to the police station," said Sylvester. "Please calm yourself."

"I thought she didn't want to leave the library undefended in case of another break-in."

"Obviously, she put me in charge," he said self-importantly. "Since Candace isn't capable enough."

"And me?" Cass raised a brow at him. "I don't like what you're implying."

"You two can argue it out." I made for the door. "I'm going to find the others—Sylvester, don't start. I was already outside the library when you were put in charge, remember?"

The owl huffed. "Nobody respects me."

I closed the door on his complaints and hurried down the steps away from the library, my mind reeling. I didn't particularly want to face Edwin's annoyance when I admitted that the suspect who I'd handed to Evangeline had met an unfortunate end, but that didn't mean I could justify keeping anything else from him. Besides, the others needed to know about Diane's demise and Laney's arrest too.

I reached the seafront and halted outside the police station. The automatic doors slid open, revealing Edwin sitting alone behind his desk. *Wait, the others left?*

Edwin saw me and sighed. "Rory, what is it this time?"

"Have you seen my aunt and cousin?"

His jaw twitched. "Yes, I have. I hope you've come to tell me you found that pendant they mentioned given that it's a valuable piece of evidence."

Ack. "No, but Diane was murdered in her cell, seemingly by another vampire."

He raised a hand. "I don't want to hear it."

"What?" Of all his possible reactions, I hadn't expected that one. "I thought you wanted me to keep you in the loop."

"It's clear that was wishful thinking on my part," he said. "Evangeline is simply unwilling to cooperate with me, and if her fellow vampires took in the prisoner, then I'm out of the equation. It'll be easier for everyone if I focus my efforts elsewhere, such as on managing the crowds attending the carnival."

"But..." I trailed off. "I wanted to warn you in case the killer is still in town. Have you seen Eric?"

"No, I have not."

Eric hadn't spoken to the police, then. As I'd thought. "I'm concerned that the Founders might target him, too, since he no longer has the pendant's protection to keep them from reading his thoughts."

"I would advise you to send Eric himself to speak to me, then." He waved me off. "Now, if you don't mind, I have work to do."

I left the police station since I didn't know what else to do. If he thought the Founders would spare him if I kept my distance, he was mistaken, but Evangeline wanted nothing more to do with my family, so I couldn't count on her to come to anyone's defence either.

Including Laney's.

I looked up and down the seafront in search of Estelle and Aunt Adelaide but saw no familiar bright-red hair among the crowds thronging the pier. Edwin did at least seem to have assigned a couple of his troll guards to keep an eye out for trouble, though, and the two grey-skinned giants made an intimidating contrast to the cheery crowds.

I made my way to the stall with the cuddly dragons and spoke to the rat shifter in charge. "Excuse me, have you seen my cousin?"

"Sure," he said. "She left a few minutes ago, with her mother."

"Where to?"

"Back to the library, I assumed."

"Are you sure—wait, where's Jet?" I'd almost forgotten my familiar had been with them too. "My familiar—a black crow—he was with Estelle."

"Huh. I didn't see him."

A chill raced down my spine, though I willed myself to stay calm as I walked away from the more crowded part of the seafront to call for my familiar.

"Jet," I called. "Jet!"

No answer came, though the level of noise surrounding the seafront would make it difficult for him to hear me. It was several minutes before I heard the answering caw of "Partner!"

Jet came zipping over to me, spraying me with droplets of water. From the bedraggled look of his feathers, he'd recently taken a swim.

I caught him in my hand. "What on earth happened to you?"

"He threw me into the sea!" said the little crow indignantly.

"Who?" More to the point, how had he ended up being separated from the others? *Where is Estelle?*

"A shifter, partner!" he squeaked. "Patrick, I heard them call him."

"Him?" I looked wildly around for the troublemaking shifter, but I saw no signs of him. "Why would he attack you?"

"Your cousin sent me to follow him, partner!"

"Estelle." She must have spotted the troublemaker and sent Jet to ensure he didn't try any more trickery, but where was she now? "Where'd she go?"

"I don't know." He beat his wings, flicking saltwater everywhere. "I followed him, but he caught me and threw me into the sea!"

"He didn't want to be followed?" I turned back to the police station. "*This* sounds like something Edwin ought to know."

I walked back to the police station and stopped in my tracks when one of Edwin's troll guards stuck out an arm and blocked my path.

"Ack." I took a step back. "Sorry. Can I help you?"

The troll peered down at me. "Didn't Edwin tell you to leave?"

"Yeah, but... my familiar was attacked." I held up the rumpled crow, who gave a pitiful squeak. The troll wouldn't be able to understand Jet's speech, so I did my best to explain. "This werewolf—Patrick, I think his name is—was making trouble at the carnival the other day. The police know who he is because he also got thrown out of the Black Dog pub, and—I think he might have been doing something illegal today, too, because he threw Jet into the sea when he followed him."

"Followed him?" The troll gave a confused blink, which I didn't entirely blame him for. "Where is he? The werewolf?"

"I don't know." I looked down at Jet, who hid himself in the hood of my cloak. "He left. Probably went home."

The police would be able to find his address if they were so inclined, but that was doubtful. While the troll continued to watch me with a puzzled expression, I spotted Cass approaching at speed.

"I thought you'd gone back to the vampires again," she said accusingly. "What's taking you so long?"

"I can't find your mother and sister anywhere," I told her. "Jet claimed they sent him to follow that werewolf guy—the one who was making trouble at the carnival the other day—and the guy threw him into the sea."

"Who? What have you done this time?" She looked up at Edwin's troll guard and closed her mouth, apparently realising that fighting with me in front of the police was not the wisest of ideas.

"The guy who tried to win about fifty of those cuddly dragons the other day," I explained. "He tried to steal from the same stall and got caught by Estelle, so I wouldn't be surprised if he was up to something illegal today too."

Cass blinked. "He stole from the carnival? Didn't my sister report him to the police?"

"She wouldn't let me tell anyone," I said. "You know what she's like—she thinks anything connected to the carnival is her responsibility."

"I'll talk sense into her." Cass made for the pier, applying a liberal use of her pointy elbows to make her way through the crowd.

"Hang on." I hastened to follow her. "I don't think she's here. Or your mum. In fact, I don't know *where* they are."

The rat shifter from the stall waved us over. "You still can't find your cousin?"

"No... have you seen that werewolf?" I asked. "The guy who won all those dragons by cheating?"

He'd also been one of my suspects for Jeffrey's murder, but there was zero chance a shifter could possibly be connected to the Founders. Right?

He blanched. "Yeah, I saw him briefly, but he didn't stick around when he saw those trolls were watching out for trouble. Thank goodness."

"When was this?" I asked.

"I dunno, maybe half an hour ago or so? Why?"

"No reason." Cass grabbed my arm and pulled me away from him, using her other elbow to part the crowd.

"Hey!" I yanked my arm free. "He might have been able to figure out where your sister is."

"No, he wouldn't have," she retaliated. "I'd say we find that shifter dude. *He* knows where they are, I guarantee it."

"Even if he does, how're we supposed to find him?" I asked. "We don't have his address."

"No." A shadow passed over her face. "But I know someone who might tell us."

"The pack chief." Cass's ex-boyfriend was one of the two sons of Chief Tarquin, leader of the local werewolf pack. While they were acquainted, that didn't mean it wouldn't be awkward if we showed up on their doorstep to ask for help... but if anyone knew exactly where that troublemaker lived, it was the leader of the werewolves.

Whether he'd tell us was another matter entirely, but I was out of any better ideas. Cass and I left the seafront and headed for the other side of town, where the local werewolf pack made their home. Jet remained hidden inside my hood the whole time instead of flying alongside me as he usually would, which further strengthened my resolve to ask that werewolf what he was playing at.

At least we didn't have to set foot near the vampires en route, though the question of Laney's fate lurked in the back of my mind. We could only deal with one crisis at a time, and it was a rarity for Cass to offer me a helping hand with anything. While we walked, I filled her in on the details of the werewolf and his antics at the carnival.

"You thought that guy was the murderer?" she asked. "Staking a vampire in the back doesn't sound much like a werewolf's kind of thing."

"I thought he might be a witness at the very least," I said. "He was near the seafront after the carnival closed for the night since he got himself kicked out of the Black Dog. I know that was hours before the murder, but I find it suspicious that he keeps coming back to the crime scene."

"No wonder." She led the way through one of the parks that covered the shifters' area of town until we emerged onto a familiar street. "Here we are."

The werewolf pack leader lived in a whitewashed house whose windows were bigger than the door as if to let in as much sunlight as possible.

I hesitated before knocking on the door. "Are you sure they'll be willing to help us out?"

"Haven't a clue."

Great. We had to at least try, if just for the sake of finding our missing family members. Besides, Patrick had to answer for throwing my familiar into the sea.

After I knocked, a tall blond werewolf answered the door, dressed in nothing but a pair of shorts as if he was about to go to the beach. Patch, brother of Cass's ex-boyfriend, eyed the pair of us in surprise.

"Hey," he said. "Er... is something up?"

"Yes." I glanced sideways at Cass, who seemed content to let me do the talking. That figured. "We're trying to find a werewolf, and since we don't know his address, we thought we'd come here."

"Who're you trying to find?"

"Patrick... something," I said. "He has a daughter, and he's been causing trouble at the carnival. He has a bit of a temper."

"I know who you mean." His nose wrinkled with disgust. "He's been in trouble with my dad a few times too. He has no respect."

"Oh, good." My shoulders slumped with relief. "I mean, it's not good, but I'm not surprised that he's been in trouble. He tried to steal from the carnival when it was closed, *and* he threw my familiar into the sea earlier."

"Oh, your sister's running the carnival." He addressed Cass. "Right?"

"We need that guy's address," she said without answering. "Preferably as quickly as possible."

"Huh?" he said. "I don't know his address by heart. I'd have to ask my dad, and I don't know that he'll give it to me without wanting to know exactly why."

"He's a thief and a troublemaker. Isn't that enough?" Cass asked. "If he doesn't talk to us, then I'll call the police, and they'll come here themselves."

"Really?" His confusion turned to seriousness. "All right, I'll tell my dad."

As he vanished into the house, I turned to Cass. "That's stretching the truth a bit. Edwin had no intention of leaving his office the last I saw of him."

"He'd change his mind if you mentioned that Estelle caught the dude stealing from the carnival," she said. "*She* should have told him."

"Yes, I know," I said. "What will bringing Edwin here achieve though? If he turns out not to know where Estelle went, then we'll hit another dead end."

"You're the one who wanted to speak to him." She looked as if she wanted to say more, but she closed her mouth when Patch reappeared.

"My dad told me that Patrick lives over at Horsetail Street on the other side of the park," Patch said. "Number seven. He also told me that if the police are on the way, he wants to talk to them too."

"He did?" I raised a brow at Cass. "What do you think?"

"I'd say we go straight there." She turned her back on the house, leaving a bemused Patch standing on the doorstep.

"Cass!" I gave Patch an apologetic look. "Sorry. I know this seems weird, but Patrick's been stirring up trouble at the carnival for a while and Estelle sent my familiar to keep an eye on him while he was at the beach earlier. Patrick reacted by throwing my familiar into the sea, so I think there's a fair chance he was up to something illegal."

"Oh." He still looked bewildered. "Why didn't you get the address from the police, then?"

"We... well, the police aren't exactly falling over themselves to come looking for him. They're busy." I didn't need to confuse and alarm him by mentioning *why* Edwin had ceased to listen to me. "With the carnival. Cass suggested coming here to ask you where to find him. Or your brother."

He blew out a breath. "Lucky it was me who answered the door, not my brother because I'm not sure he'd have been as willing to help her if the police *weren't* involved. I won't tell my dad that, don't worry."

"Thanks." I backed up a step to avoid letting Cass out of my sight. "I'd better catch up to her."

"Wise idea. I'll see if I can convince my brother to back you up in case it turns ugly."

"Wait." I hurried after Cass and caught her up at the park. "Cass, slow down. Wouldn't you rather we had backup?"

"You're my backup." Without slowing, she marched onward, leaving me in the dust.

I fished a reluctant Jet out of my hood. "Jet, can you fly back and tell Edwin where we are? This way you get to avoid Patrick."

Jet shivered. "Of course, partner!"

He took flight, while I prepared to face the wolves. Or wolf, rather. The shifter had given me bad vibes from the start, but might he be worse than a petty thief? Might he know where my cousin was?

Cass was already hammering on the door to one of the houses by the time I reached her. Several tense moments later, the door opened, revealing Patrick himself. He was dressed in a sloppy T-shirt and tracksuit bottoms, and his lip curled in a snarl when he saw me. "I know you."

"You tried to drown my familiar," were the first words out of my mouth. "Why?"

"*You* sent that crow to follow me, didn't you?" he growled. "Thought I wouldn't notice?"

"No, I didn't send him." My instincts screamed at me to run, but the need to find my missing family members kept me rooted to the spot. "My cousin did. Where is she?"

"What do you mean, where is she?" The hairs rose on my arms as he moved into the doorway, his bulk filling the frame. "Back at that carnival of hers, obviously. What gives you the right to come to my house and start asking me questions?"

"Because you're the last person who saw my sister," said Cass, "and the police are on their way here to arrest you for murder."

"Murder!" He yelped the word. "What? Someone murdered your sister?"

"No!" I interjected, wondering why Cass thought that freaking out an already agitated werewolf was a wise idea. "Someone murdered a vampire the other night, and you're wanted for questioning as an eyewitness." I was improvising, but Cass's slight nod indicated that she'd planned to make the same accusation.

To my surprise, the werewolf's anger shifted to panic. "I'm not a witness. I didn't see nothing."

"That means you did." Cass's tone gained a hint of triumph. "You're lying."

"I didn't lay a finger on that vampire!"

"Then what about a stake?" My heart began to race. *He was there.* My hunch had been right all along. "Did you stake that vampire in the back?"

"No," he snarled. "You'd better get away from my house. I'm innocent."

"Are you now?" Patch walked up behind us, hardly out of breath despite having presumably run here directly from his house. "Sounds to me like you've been caught red-handed."

"I didn't kill nobody!" His voice dropped to a growl that sounded more like a wolf than a human, and I dragged Cass away from the doorway in case he did turn into a wolf and attack us.

Patch stepped into our place, facing him without any

fear. "Tell me the truth, or else my father will be the next to pay you a visit."

"I've no idea what those witches are talking about." Patrick glowered at us. "They're lying."

"You're a thief and a liar yourself," Cass said. "And possibly a murderer too. What really happened between you and that vampire the other night?"

"We argued," he muttered. "At the pub. He left before I did, and then I got kicked out. And..."

"And what?" asked Cass.

"And... someone killed him." Patrick took in a breath. His expression had lost some of its anger and instead showed a hint of fear. "It happened too fast for me to see who it was. I was pretty drunk anyway, and they moved so quickly that they were gone before I could blink. And then... then that guy was lying dead on the beach."

"Another vampire killed him?" I concluded. "Are you being truthful?"

"Of course I am," he growled. "After, I tried to get back into the pub, but they wouldn't let me, so I left. That's all."

"Then why did you throw my familiar into the sea?"

"The crow?" The anger returned to his voice. "Because he was following me. Does there need to be a reason?"

"Yes, because you're the last person who saw my sister," Cass snarled right back at him. "Tell me where she is."

"I don't know!" His face flushed bright red. "I haven't seen her. That is the truth."

"I think he's being honest this time," I said to Cass in an undertone. "He didn't even speak to Estelle."

Nor would he have a reason to take her.

"One more question," Cass said to Patrick. "Ever heard of the Founders?"

"The who?"

"Never mind." She swept away from his house, leaving me in charge of apologising to Patch. Again.

"Don't worry about it," he said. "You go and find Estelle. You think she's in trouble, right?"

"Yeah... I did send my familiar to fetch the police after all, so hopefully, Edwin will be along soon."

A growl sounded. "He'd better not."

In a flash of fur, Patrick shifted into a wolf. Patch was ready, though, and when he turned into a wolf of equal size, he blocked the doorway, barring the other wolf from running after us.

"Let's move," Cass muttered. "I don't see that guy escaping from the pack leader."

"I hope Edwin is ready." I also hoped the other werewolves would be able to keep him restrained while we went in search of our missing relatives because we wouldn't be able to come back and help.

Not if Estelle and Aunt Adelaide were in as much trouble as I feared.

14

Cass and I walked at speed back to the beach. I knew we wouldn't find Aunt Adelaide or Estelle there, but the foremost of our dwindling options was to search the area where they'd last been and hope that someone had spotted them.

"How can they have just vanished without anyone seeing?" I remarked aloud as we walked. "Especially right by the crowds on the pier?"

"Those vampires move fast."

My chest contracted at her casual acknowledgement of the fear I hadn't voiced aloud. "Do they make a habit of kidnapping people in broad daylight?"

"I wouldn't put anything past them."

Meaning the Founders. I wouldn't, either, and anyone who could stab another vampire in the back without being caught certainly had the skills necessary to capture two members of our family. Yet I had a hard time believing Estelle or Aunt Adelaide would have surrendered without a fight, which made it even less likely that nobody had seen.

As we neared the seafront, I slowed my pace. "Cass, wait. I know someone who might have seen them."

"Who?"

"Eric." Why hadn't I thought of him earlier? "He lives just down here. We can ask him."

"Fine." She swivelled on her heel and waited impatiently while I mentally retraced my steps to find the right house. I might be on the wrong track entirely, but it wasn't impossible that Estelle and Aunt Adelaide had decided to pay Eric a visit to ask more questions. Hardly anyone was in this part of town, either, and the silence struck me as ominous despite the distant cheery sounds of the carnival carried on the breeze.

When I knocked on the door to Eric's house, there was a long silence before the door nudged open a fraction. Eric's frightened face peered out. "Rory. Hi."

"Have you seen my aunt and cousin?"

He lowered his gaze. "Yeah... I'm sorry."

My skin chilled. "Why? Where are they?"

"They... they came here to talk to me." He whispered the words. "And... and they were ambushed. It happened so quickly."

"Ambushed by whom?" Dread choked my breath. "The Founders took them. Didn't they?"

"I don't know where they went." His voice trembled. "I wish there was something I could have done—"

"Save your snivelling," Cass said. "Let's go, Rory."

"Stay hidden," I told Eric, my heart hammering against my chest. "If I were you, I'd lie low."

"That was the plan." He exhaled. "I'm sorry. There was nothing I could do. I don't even have the pendant."

"I know." That we'd taken it off him couldn't have

helped, but it also wouldn't have been much use against the Founders on its own.

The mental image brought a rush of delayed panic as the extent of our dilemma hit me. If my aunt and cousin had been taken outside of Ivory Beach, then they might well be halfway across the country by now. How were we supposed to find them?

Cass waved a hand in front of my face. "Rory, get a grip. We're wasting our time by sticking around here when we could be finding them."

"Where?" I queried. "We don't even know where the Founders are based."

Laney might, but our chances of rescuing her from Evangeline's clutches were slim.

Cass paced away from me, heading towards the beach. "That Eric guy doesn't know either. The Founders wouldn't have left him alone if he did."

"We should tell the police, then." I walked fast to keep up with her. "Granted, Edwin might already be on his way to the werewolves."

"Edwin isn't going to be of any use either," she said. "He doesn't know the vampires like we do."

"We?" I echoed. "You mean me. Right?"

"You have personal experience negotiating with them."

"You mean experience in getting kidnapped by the Founders myself," I corrected. "There was no negotiation involved."

"I thought you'd leap at the chance to break your friend out of Evangeline's dungeon."

"What?" I said, disarmed. "No, I'm not breaking in. Do you think Evangeline would let someone sneak into her home twice in a day?"

Assuming the person who'd killed Diane had come from

outside, but Evangeline thought Laney herself had. *What a mess.*

Cass grunted and fell silent, which I assumed meant she agreed. After a long pause, she turned to me. "How did she manage to keep her thoughts hidden from Evangeline in the first place? Isn't the head vampire supposed to be able to break into anyone's mind?"

"Theoretically," I said, "but it depends on the individual, and she doesn't like admitting anyone might have an edge over her."

"You mean the Founders?" She raised her head. "That's it. Mortimer Vale is on the same level as Evangeline, and he's the one who turned Laney. I should have guessed."

"Don't speak so loudly," I hissed. "In fact, I wouldn't even *think* that while you're within reach of Evangeline."

Cass gave a low whistle. "Now I get why Evangeline locked up your friend. It's lucky for her that Mortimer Vale is locked up somewhere he can't exert his control over her."

My stomach turned over. "What?"

"You didn't know vampire sires have influence over anyone they turn?" she asked. "Look, Rory, Vale can't do anything while he's in prison. Forget I said anything."

Easier said than done. If Mortimer Vale ever walked free again, then Laney would be in more trouble than I'd ever imagined. It was bad enough that he was to blame for her being able to outmanoeuvre Evangeline. *She won't cave in and set her free, but I have to try.*

"Laney knows where the Founders hold their gatherings." I returned to the dilemma at hand. "That means we need to convince Evangeline to let us talk to her. Granted, that leaves the problem of how we're supposed to break into the property of one of the Founders without losing our heads."

"Breaking in might not be necessary," Cass said. "The Founders don't seem picky about who they let into their gatherings. Not the humans, anyway."

"I'm best friends with someone who murdered two of them," I pointed out. "I can protect my mind from being read up to a point, but not against someone as strong as Mortimer Vale."

She rolled her eyes. "I'll go, then."

"What?" I stopped in my tracks. "No way."

"Nobody knows me," she pointed out. "I wouldn't be recognised."

"Cass, we're related. We even look similar."

"None of the Founders have actually set eyes on you except the three who are in jail, have they?" she queried. "Same with me. It's worth a shot."

I opened my mouth to reply, and a flicker of movement caught my eye. We'd reached the seafront, but this end of the beach was deserted compared to the other side where the crowds had gathered near the pier. As the breeze off the ocean brought a faint salty tang to the air, I had the sudden chilling certainty that the two of us weren't alone.

Cass shot me a frown when I reached for my wand. Another shadow flitted in the corner of my vision, and certainty seized me. There was a vampire nearby.

I turned on my heel and fired off a freeze-frame spell that whipped past the vampire who was tailing us. Cass seized her wand, too, but her spell missed as the vampire moved so fast he might as well have been made of smoke.

"Show yourself." Cass's second spell missed its target, too, as did mine. It was like trying to throw a rock at a ghost. While I'd brought a small bag of firedust as well as my Biblio-Witch Inventory, neither of those things would be of much use unless I could slow down our adversary.

As I scanned the road running parallel to the beach, I ran through a mental inventory of all the spells I'd learned. My mind snagged on Aunt Candace's last lesson. I'd hardly practised the lullaby charm she'd taught me, but she'd said it would be as effective on vampires as it was on humans. And thanks to her using me as a guinea pig, I had an all-too-clear memory of how to cast the spell.

I twirled my wand, and a series of musical notes poured from the end. Cass swayed on the spot, and I hastily jerked my wand sideways, not wanting to knock her out cold instead of the vampire. *Where is he?*

Movement stirred, and the vampire appeared, his hands covering his ears. To no avail since his enhanced senses would work against him for once. When I met his eyes, recognition flared.

Joseph. The vampire I'd spoken to the last time I'd visited Evangeline's house, the one who'd demonstrated an irrational dislike of Laney.

Cass's next freeze-frame spell hit him square in the face, causing him to slow to a complete standstill. "Rory, turn off that racket or else you'll have to carry him alone."

I belatedly realised my wand had started emitting a noise that sounded more like a siren than a lullaby and hastily undid the spell. The vampire remained frozen for an instant before he recovered, making a break for it down a nearby street.

Cass swore and gave chase. The spell must have still been partly in effect because her next spell hit him square in the back, sending the vampire flying headlong into a wall. Brick cracked, but vampires were made of stronger stuff than regular people. Joseph staggered backwards, a growl slipping between his teeth.

Cass pointed her wand at him again. "Where do you think you're going?"

I ran to her side and spotted several wooden stakes lying scattered at Joseph's feet. "You're the one who's been staking people?"

Of course. He'd been inside Evangeline's home already, so he'd had ample opportunity to target Diane while she'd been unconscious in her cell. Why though?

He glared. "You're lucky I didn't do the same to you since you brought them here."

"Who?" Then it clicked. "The Founders. You're not with them?"

"Of course I'm not with them," he growled. "I'm trying to keep them from infiltrating this town like they've done to so many others, but your family is making that impossible."

He'd killed Jeffrey *and* Diane. Not because he was with the Founders himself, but because he wanted to keep them out.

"You were going after Eric." Cass's voice shook with anger. "Weren't you? You were going to stake him too."

"Is that true?" He'd even go so far as to murder a human who'd never even *met* the Founders? "Wait... what did you do to my cousin and aunt?"

"Nothing whatsoever." He made to run, but Cass flicked her wand and sent him flying headfirst into the wall again.

"Use that lullaby spell, Rory," she ordered.

Somewhat surprised that she'd ask me to help after I'd nearly knocked her out cold the last time, I waved my wand. My spell conjured a string of notes that were slightly more pleasant to the ears than my previous attempt, and Joseph swayed, falling unconscious against the wall.

"It worked." I took a step back when Cass gave a flick of

her wand and levitated Joseph's unconscious body into the air. "Wait, where are you taking him?"

"To the one person he might spill the truth to."

In other words, Evangeline. That was our only option, really, but if he'd been lying—if he'd been the one who'd taken Estelle and Aunt Adelaide—why would she lift a finger to help us?

Or maybe he'd been truthful. After all, why would he have targeted my aunt and cousin and not Laney—or me? The pair of us had been more to blame for the Founders' presence in the town than any of my family members had. I'd have to wait until he woke up to ask him, so I walked on towards the seafront and hoped that the carnival was too much of a distraction for anyone to question why Cass and I were levitating an unconscious vampire through a public street.

Strangely enough, nobody did flag us down. We did catch a few confused stares on our way across the town square and up the high street, but Cass's constant glare ensured nobody stopped to ask us any questions. We reached the church faster than I'd expected and without being challenged either.

I knocked, and this time an unfamiliar female vampire answered the door.

"I need to talk to Evangeline," I said. "It's urgent."

"She told me you'd say that," she said dismissively. "And the answer's no."

"Tell her the Founders came to Ivory Beach, and we have the murderer she's looking for."

The vampire vanished in a flash and returned with Evangeline so rapidly I had to wonder if she'd been watching the door the whole time.

"Where are the Founders?" Evangeline demanded. "If

you're lying to me again, Aurora, then you'll join your friend in the dungeon."

"I don't know where they are, but he might." I indicated Joseph's hovering form above Cass's head. "This guy's been killing anyone connected with the Founders, including Jeffrey and Diane. He was on his way to kill Eric next when we caught him."

Cass flicked her wand, and Joseph's body crashed to the ground in front of Evangeline. He groaned, stirring, while Evangeline leaned over him. "Is it true? Did you kill my prisoner?"

He raised his head to glare at Cass and me and spoke in a slurred voice. "This is her fault, not mine."

"He thought he was stopping the Founders," I explained. "He was on his way to Eric's house when we caught him, but Estelle and Aunt Adelaide are missing, and he says he doesn't know where they are."

She pursed her lips, looking down at him. "He spoke true when he claimed not to know their location, but I cannot allow him to live."

Joseph rolled upright, but Evangeline was ready. Her hand struck his face, hard, and he collapsed into a heap once more.

I flinched. "Is he... dead?"

"No," she said. "He might wish otherwise when he wakes up since he forgot his place among us, and he will pay the price for it."

I shivered. Vampire justice was merciless at best. "If Aunt Adelaide and Estelle aren't here, then... then the Founders must have taken them elsewhere. Is there any chance we can talk to Laney?"

"No," she answered. "She needs time to think on her

transgressions, and I will not allow her to escape unpunished."

I'd hoped Cass would back me up, but she remained silent. "I... I wouldn't ask this of you if we had a choice in the matter, but we don't know the location of the Founders' hideout."

"If Elaine knows their location, then I can easily get that information from her," said Evangeline. "You can deal with the rest yourself."

"The rest?" I echoed. "I don't understand what you mean."

Her teeth showed as she gave one of her slightly terrifying smiles. "Why, Aurora, I think you do. If you ask any more of me, then we will have to make another arrangement."

I gaped at her for a moment. By "arrangement," I assumed she meant she'd only help me to find my family if I agreed to owe her another favour. Did she want me indebted to her forever?

"The answer is no." Cass finally spoke. "No more deals."

"I believe I was asking Aurora, not you."

I tensed. "Evangeline, this isn't between the two of us anymore. The Founders are a legitimate threat to all of us. Just the thought of them being in town was enough for one of your own people to turn against you. I'll gladly take on responsibility for rescuing Estelle and Aunt Adelaide, but we can't stop the Founders single-handedly, and I also can't guarantee the ripple effects won't end up back here if we fail."

For a heartbeat, I expected her to refuse, to slam the door on us—but the truth in my words won out.

Evangeline's jaw twitched. "You are both lucky that the

Founders are the ones most deserving of my wrath. I will go and speak to Elaine."

She vanished from sight in a blink.

Cass stirred. "Elaine? Really?"

"Yes, why?" I wasn't surprised that Cass couldn't have cared less if Laney walked free or not, but we had another issue to consider. "Cass, I meant it when I said we're too recognisable to walk into one of the Founders' gatherings through the front doors. So is Evangeline, so even if she *does* offer to help us, it won't exactly be a subtle way to stage a rescue mission. We're likely to be outnumbered too."

"I can think of someone who might be able to help." Her attention focused on a spot somewhere behind me.

"Who?" I turned. Saw who she meant. "Oh no."

"Oh yes." Aunt Candace grinned. "My moment has come."

15

"How long have you been listening to us?" I asked Aunt Candace. To further my confusion, Jet perched on her shoulder. My familiar must have returned to the library after he'd sent Edwin after the werewolves, but how on earth had my aunt known we'd be at the vampires' home?

"Long enough," she replied. "Did you expect me not to notice you levitating an unconscious vampire across the square?"

"Yes," said Cass. "You're usually paying no attention to anything that isn't between the pages of a book."

"The cheek of it," she said. "Tell me everything at once."

"There's no time," I stepped away from the church, conscious of the closed door inches away from us and the vampires who might be listening on the other side. "The Founders took Aunt Adelaide and Estelle, and I'm pretty sure we're the only people who might be able to save them."

"I imagine our illustrious leading vampire is willing to help," she said.

"Not quite," I said. "Even if she is, I'm pretty sure

directly getting involved in a fight with the Founders would be more likely to end up with us dead. Though our only other option is to sneak in without being caught, which is about as likely as Sylvester developing a conscience."

"Not if you allow me to create a distraction," she said. "Go on, tell me everything while we wait for our prickly friend to return."

I cast a wary look at the church door, but Evangeline didn't appear and neither did anyone else. I dreaded to think of how her conversation with Laney might be going, so to distract myself, I gave Aunt Candace a rundown of how we'd gone from looking for Estelle and Aunt Adelaide to accidentally finding the killer.

"Tricky vampires," she said. "It would be my pleasure to throw a wrench in those Founders' sinister plans."

"Someone has to stay in the library," I told her. "If all three of us go, then we'll have to leave Sylvester in charge."

"He'll be fine," said Cass. "He's a genius loci, right? He won't let the Founders get in."

"They've got in before," I reminded her, wishing she'd keep her voice down. "He's probably the one who took Eric's pendant, but I doubt they'd be able to read his mind anyway since he isn't human."

Cass reached into her pocket. "Actually..."

I swore under my breath. "Seriously? You took the pendant?"

"It seemed easier than listening to you and Laney argue over who to give it to."

I sighed. "You do realise you won't be able to hide that from Evangeline?"

"I think she has other problems, don't you?"

Typical. Cass must have eavesdropped on our conversation with Eric and then feigned ignorance, but that was a minor consideration in the face of what was to come.

Evangeline returned, displaying no signs of having heard us. "Elaine has told me the address of the Founder who is most likely to have taken your family members. It seems that the Founders will be hosting one of their gatherings this evening."

"For whom?" I asked. "If it's for the Founders only, then we'll never be able to get in."

"No," she said. "The Founders allow any humans into their gatherings, or so your friend claims."

"That doesn't mean they'll let *us* in."

"Then I'd advise you to formulate a plan," she said. "I cannot accompany you into the Founders' base, but if you return here in an hour, I will give you the directions to the location. I intend to discuss the matter with my fellow vampires in the meantime."

That seemed suspiciously generous of her. When she vanished into the church, though, my doubts came surging back. "Does anyone actually have a plan that won't result in us all ending up dead?"

"I do," said Aunt Candace. "I'll lead the way into the Founders' gathering and distract the hosts by telling them I'm researching a book. It's true enough."

"Unless they read your mind."

"They won't find anything useful in there," she said confidently. "I have decades of pointless information stored inside my head."

"She has a point," said Cass. "I'd say it's worth a shot."

Jet flew to my shoulder. "I'll help, partner!"

"I don't want you in harm's way either." I could hardly believe that we had to depend upon Aunt Candace of all people to provide enough of a cover to sneak into the

Founders' event, but what other option did we have? Cass had the pendant to keep her thoughts hidden, but while I'd been practising for months, my nervousness over Laney and the others would make it more likely that my thoughts would give me away. It didn't help that none of us was familiar with the location. Laney had been there before, but thanks to Evangeline's stubbornness, we'd have to go in without her direct guidance. We didn't have a choice.

Xavier might have been able to help, but his boss would never allow him to step so far out of his role as the Reaper to infiltrate a vampire gathering and potentially get himself captured or killed. His ability to walk through walls would come in handy, undeniably, but was it worth antagonising the Grim Reaper?

While we waited for Evangeline's return, I paced over to the cemetery entrance and then waited outside as if I could conjure up Xavier without needing to go through his boss.

My blood turned to water when the shadowy figure of the Grim Reaper appeared behind the gate as if my thoughts genuinely *had* conjured him out of nowhere. "Ah... sorry. I'm—"

"Planning to do something foolish, I know." His words were as cold as an arctic tundra. "The answer is no, you may *not* take my apprentice with you on your ill-advised rescue mission."

My mouth fell open. "Were you eavesdropping on us?"

"You forget it was I who reaped the soul of the imprisoned vampire, Aurora," he said. "I have been watching the situation, and when I saw you and your cousin carrying that unconscious vampire, I found myself intrigued enough to follow you. You brought him down by yourself, did you?"

"Yes..." Why had he brought that up? He didn't sound impressed, but I wouldn't be able to tell if he was since his voice had no inflection to speak of at the best of times. "He's the one who killed those two vampires. Did you already know?"

"No, I did not," he said. "My concern is with the dead alone—the truly dead, not those pale imitations of the living."

Ouch. I was glad Evangeline wasn't around to hear his snub, even if it was kind of accurate. "I didn't expect you to let Xavier come with me, but can't I at least tell him where I'm going?"

"No," he said. "He will want to prevent you from leaving. I imagine listening to his protests is not as tiresome to you as it is to me, but you do not wish to be further delayed, do you?"

"Definitely not," answered Cass, who'd followed me to the gate. "We don't need the Reaper's help."

"That's not your call to make." I turned to her, but she was looking at the Reaper without so much as a hint of fear in her expression. I wished I knew what was going on in her head. Or maybe I didn't want to know.

"No, it's the Grim Reaper's call," she said. "He said no, and he's right. Do you want to spend all evening arguing over the pros and cons of storming the vampires' base?"

"No, but that wouldn't be an issue if Xavier was allowed to come with us," I said. "It doesn't contradict his role as a Reaper, does it?"

"It does," said the Grim Reaper. "I will only allow him to leave my side if there is a vampire's soul in need of Reaping. It's up to you if you want to arrange that."

"You're joking." Nope, he wasn't. "If I die out there, then I can guarantee he'll see to it that you regret keeping him from coming with me."

"Then you'd better not die, Aurora."

In a sweep of his cloak, he vanished into the shadows.

I turned on Cass. "Thanks a bunch. You didn't need to encourage him to be even more of a stick-in-the-mud than he already is."

"I didn't need to try," she retaliated. "We already have more than enough people to stage a rescue mission. Any more would draw too much suspicion."

"Xavier can make himself unseen, in case you've forgotten." Instead, we'd have three humans against a dozen or more vampires.

Cass made no reply, and despite her confident words, her manner grew terser as the hour drew nearer. Only Aunt Candace seemed mildly cheerful as if she'd been waiting for such an opportunity.

"None of you is dressed appropriately," she chided, looking me and Cass up and down. "This is a high-class event, isn't it?"

"I'll handle it." Cass lifted her wand. "Keep still, both of you."

Before anyone could raise an objection, she pointed her wand at me and then Aunt Candace in turn. A breeze lifted my hair, and I looked down and saw my cloak had been replaced with a black dress, while a fancy shoulder bag took the place of my everyday one. Somehow, she'd even transported my Biblio-Witch Inventory into the shoulder bag without even taking it out of my pocket, which was impressive.

"I didn't know you knew spells like that," I remarked.

"Of course I do." She applied another spell to her hair, which restyled itself into curls. "I don't usually spend my free time infiltrating vampire gatherings."

"You don't say." Aunt Candace gave a twirl on the spot, admiring her own flowery dress. "Perfect."

That was one problem taken care of, but how would we get to the gathering itself? Evangeline had promised to give us the address, but that didn't mean she had any intention of coming with us. She'd be wiser not to, as the Founders would certainly know who she was.

Aunt Candace volunteered Cass to go back to the library to tell Sylvester where we were going, correctly guessing that if she went herself, then Cass and I might leave without her. Cass returned within a few minutes with the news that Sylvester intended to fortify the library in our absence.

"We'll have a hell of a time getting back in," she said. "He's not taking any chances."

"He isn't volunteering to help us out though." Not that there was much the owl could do to help us outside of the library. His abilities were severely hindered without the library's magic, and even our own biblio-witch magic wouldn't work as well as it usually did. I'd have to rely on my wand.

Evangeline emerged from the church and gave the three of us an appraising look. "That'll do. You won't stand out now you're dressed like that."

"Are you coming with us?" I hesitantly asked, noticing movement behind the door that suggested several other vampires were waiting in the wings. "I know you won't be able to come into the gathering itself, but if you want to catch the Founders midplan, this might be the best chance you have."

"I will give you half an hour," she said. "If you haven't rescued your family members in that time, then I cannot promise you'll be safe from the consequences when my fellow vampires and myself storm the Founders' headquarters."

My blood chilled. "Half an hour? It'll take longer than that just to get there."

"I intend to walk, but I imagine you have a more practical method."

Ah. She meant magic, but transportation spells were more liable to go wrong if used to travel to a location none of us had been to before.

"What's the address?" Aunt Candace asked.

"The house is simply called Ridgeway House." Evangeline smiled, exposing her teeth. "I wish you the best of luck."

That's it? I raised a brow at Cass, but Aunt Candace pulled out her Biblio-Witch Inventory. "I imagine that picturing Adelaide and Estelle in our mind's eye will get us to the right place."

"We don't want to land in the middle of the Founders' house," I pointed out. "It's not exactly a stealthy approach, is it?"

"I can guarantee the Founders will have put up defences against people using spells to get into their gatherings." Cass pulled out her Biblio-Witch Inventory too. "In all likelihood, we'll land outside the gates."

"I *hope* you're right." If not, then we'd lose the element of surprise and possibly our heads too. Though given that there was a fight ahead of us no matter how we got in, a peaceful entry had always been a long shot.

I opened my own Biblio-Witch Inventory and skimmed down the page in search of the right word—*travel*. Pressing my fingertip to the word, I pictured my aunt and cousin in my mind's eye with all the focus I could muster.

Here goes nothing.

The church vanished, Ivory Beach itself vanished, and both were replaced with a deserted country lane. Jet cawed in surprise, while I looked up at an unruffled Cass and a triumphant Aunt Candace. The country lane was bordered by fields on either side, but a gravel path bisected two fields, leading up to a large house.

"This is the place." Aunt Candace sauntered towards the gravel path.

I put my Biblio-Witch Inventory into my shoulder bag and followed her, hoping the Founders wouldn't search us upon entry. Our Biblio-Witch Inventories would be a dead giveaway as to our identities, but my aunt and cousin were somewhere in that house.

We had to get them out.

As we made our way down the gravel path, I kept both eyes open for any signs of movement. When we rounded a corner past a hedge, I spied several well-dressed figures gathering at the far end of the path near the house.

"Evangeline isn't here," I murmured. "How long did she say we had? Half an hour?"

The place was massive. We'd be hard-pressed to search every room in that short a time frame, especially if the Founders had taken great pains to ensure their guests didn't wander out of bounds.

"Not to worry." Aunt Candace strode into the lead. "I'm sure the Founders will be willing to help someone who expresses an interest in joining their cause."

Oh boy. *That* was her plan? It might even work, but she must realise the gravity of the risk she was taking by lying to the Founders.

"Fine, but if you drop a single hint that we're here for anything other than innocent reasons, we're all dead."

"I'm no fool," said Aunt Candace. "I might remind you that my mind is full of many fascinating things I can distract them with."

That meant it was up to Cass and me to search the

house. I looked down at my familiar, who'd perched on my shoulder, trembling a little.

"Jet, can you fly up to the house and look for the others?" I whispered. "We need to know which room they're in and if anyone's guarding them. Come and tell us as soon as you find them, but try not to draw any attention."

"Yes, partner!" He flew off towards the dark shape of the house, while the rest of us continued on foot. At least a small crow would be inconspicuous, and if the Founders had been recruiting witches and wizards to join their cause, it surely wouldn't be that odd for someone to bring their familiar to their gathering.

The path gave way to a driveway that sloped uphill to the house's doorstep. A gate barred the way around the side of the house, and only the front entrance appeared to be in use. If we maintained the stealthy approach, we'd have to get out the same way we came in.

Yeah, right. Stealth isn't going to be an option for long. Especially when Evangeline showed up.

That didn't mean I could count on her to come to our rescue if we ended up in trouble. The figures I'd seen on the path must have gone into the house because nobody else appeared to be outside and a lone man watched us from the doorstep. Thin and pale, he looked as if a stiff breeze would knock him over. *He's got to be human.*

"Here for the gathering?" asked the man in a slurred voice that suggested he'd either been bitten by a vampire recently or had been drinking. Or possibly both.

"Absolutely," said Aunt Candace. "I'm here to express an interest in joining your cause. Is there someone I can talk to?"

"Of course." He shuffled out of the way, leaving a clear path for us to enter the house.

We stepped into a red-carpeted hallway, where a pair of oak doors opened on our right into a wide hall with smooth wooden floors. Vampires and humans alike mingled in small groups, dressed in finery. Opulence surrounded us on all sides, and the crystal chandelier overhead dazzled my eyes, reflecting in the wine glasses carried by dazed-looking staff. By the opaque contents, most of them did not contain regular wine. *Lovely.*

"More guests!" A man appeared in front of us, tall and dark-haired with elegantly carved features. "Excellent. I am your host, Carlos Verdant."

He's the one who owns this house? I hastened to focus my attention on the wall in case any stray thoughts slipped out, while Aunt Candace put on a broad smile. "I am *delighted* to meet you, Mr Verdant. May I ask you some questions?"

"Here we go," Cass muttered in my ear, while our aunt walked away with the host, chattering in his ear. "He knows where they are, I bet."

"Keep it down." I tensed when a petite Asian woman with a vampire's pointed fangs stepped in front of the pair of us, interest gleaming in her eyes.

"Sisters, are you?" she asked.

"No, cousins." I attempted to edge around her, but trying to dodge a vampire was like trying to walk across a piano without waking a toddler. In other words, impossible.

"I don't recall seeing either of you before," she said.

"I've been here once." To my alarm, Cass lifted the pendant from around her neck to show to the woman. "I've attended one of your gatherings before. It's where I got this."

What was she thinking? If she was trying to bluff her way into the vampires' good graces, I wished she'd told me beforehand so I could play along more convincingly. As it was, I held both my breath and my tongue while the vampire eyed the pendant with even more interest.

"You must know Carlos personally, then," she said to Cass. "If he has you on his list for a promotion."

Promotion. An interesting way to refer to being turned into a vampire. I suppressed a shudder, and to my alarm, her attention turned to me. "And you?"

"I... I'm new to this," I said. "I've met Jeffrey. He used to come to your gatherings."

"Oh, yes," she said. "I hear he met with an unfortunate accident."

How did she know? Had someone from Ivory Beach been passing on information? Diane hadn't known, but it made perfect sense that the Founders had other informants.

"Yes, it's tragic," I bluffed. "There was another, too... Diane. Is she here?"

"No, I haven't seen her," said the vampire. "Perhaps she decided to stay at home."

Cass trod on my foot. Biting back a wince, I looked over my shoulder at her and spotted Jet hovering near the large window at the front of the hall, flapping his wings in an effort to get my attention. It wouldn't be long before someone noticed him, but the vampire had already noticed my attention slip. "Is something wrong?"

Cass stepped in. "She's new to this, like she said. I think she needs to get some air."

Thanks for that, Cass. I gave a surreptitious scan of the area for Aunt Candace, who'd vanished. She hadn't gone off with Carlos Verdant alone, had she?

"Yes," I said. "I do. It's been nice meeting you."

I crossed the room to the door, hoping Jet would take the hint to follow me. Heart racing, I walked out into the corridor to wait for him to find a way in.

A long, tense couple of minutes later, Jet flitted into the hall and landed on my shoulder.

"You found them?" I breathed.

"Yes, partner!" he squeaked in my ear. "They're upstairs, in the central room facing the back lawn."

Oh boy. "Where are the stairs? Is there—?"

I trailed off when movement nearby indicated that I wasn't alone. None other than Carlos Verdant stood watching me, his expression politely incredulous.

"Please excuse me," he said. "You have an interesting choice of companion."

"He's my familiar." No sense in pretending otherwise.

"Ah, a good choice," he said. "You do know that becoming a vampire will involve surrendering your connection to your familiar as well as your magical powers?"

I stiffened, unable to hide my shock at how frankly he'd spoken. Was being chosen to be turned into a vampire really that straightforward a process?

He tilted his head. "You don't want to turn."

Ack. I'd given too much away in my reaction. "I'm considering. Losing my familiar and my magic is hard to think about. Have you seen my aunt?"

"She's gone to... ah, powder her nose," she said.

"That's right." I seized on the excuse. "I was looking for the bathroom too. Is it upstairs?"

"Upstairs?" he echoed. "No... it's just down the corridor, on the right."

He pointed, and I nodded with feigned gratitude. "Thanks. I'll be right back."

I sensed him watching me as I walked away. Jet clung to my shoulder, his little body trembling.

"I'm not really going to turn into one of them," I whispered to him. "Where's my aunt?"

"There, partner!" He pointed with a foot to an alcove in which my aunt lurked, looking distinctly uncomfortable.

"Are you all right?" I asked her.

She glared. "That vampire needs to learn to keep his hands to himself."

I shot an alarmed look over my shoulder, but Carlos Verdant hadn't followed me. *Good.* "Aunt Candace—they're upstairs. The others are. Jet said they're locked in the central room facing the back lawn."

"Upstairs?" She shuffled out of the alcove. "I just went past some stairs, but they were blocked."

"Wait—we have to tell Cass." I turned to Jet. "Can you find my cousin?"

"Yes, partner." He swooped back down the corridor, while I followed Aunt Candace around a corner. Soon, we came to a wide, carpeted staircase that had been cordoned off with a rope.

"Wait a moment." I reached out to stop her as she moved towards the rope. "There might be defensive spells—Aunt Candace!"

My aunt ignored me, lifting the rope and ducking underneath. When she strode up the staircase as if she lived here, I groaned inwardly. Did she expect *me* to distract anyone who might come past? If Carlos Verdant had got handsy with her, I didn't exactly blame her for wanting to rescue the others sooner rather than later, but she couldn't possibly expect him not to notice her sneaking around upstairs.

Jet returned seconds later. "Cass went off alone, partner!"

Oh no. "Which way?"

"Through another door, partner!" he squeaked. "I think she wants to go upstairs too."

"Right." Of course she did. "I guess it's up to us to cause a diversion—"

An unfamiliar male voice came from the top of the stairs. "You can't be up here. Who are you?"

Uh-oh. I threw caution to the wind and lifted the rope. After ducking underneath, I hurried up the stairs and came to a stop when I saw that Aunt Candace had run straight into a peeved-looking male vampire with a mohawk.

"Excuse me!" She attempted to sidestep him. "I need to powder my nose. We humans are more delicate than you vampires, you know."

The vampire moved to block her path. "The bathroom is downstairs."

"Right, right." She swung around, almost hitting the vampire in the face with her elbow in the process, while I grabbed my wand and cast an unseen spell on myself. The spell wouldn't work as effectively on a vampire's sharp senses, but I only needed to win myself a few seconds.

While the vampire watched my aunt, I cast the lullaby charm on him. Musical notes swirled from the end of my wand and wrapped around the vampire, who swayed drowsily before slumping against the wall.

"I knew you could master that spell," said Aunt Candace. "I'll have you know, I had this handled."

"Sure you did," I replied. "Help me move him into an empty room. It won't be long before the others notice he's missing."

All I could do was hope the other vampires' sensitive hearing hadn't already picked up on the noise. There didn't appear to be anyone else upstairs, but one of these rooms contained my aunt and cousin, and I hadn't a clue which direction faced the back garden.

After Aunt Candace and I had moved the vampire into

an empty room, I spied Cass, who approached from the opposite side of the corridor.

"We weren't *all* supposed to come upstairs," she said.

"Speak for yourself," I said. "Aunt Candace, can you create a diversion downstairs so nobody follows us?"

She closed the door on the unconscious vampire. "Even I can't distract a dozen people at once, Aurora."

"And I can't put them all to sleep." To my alarm, voices drifted up from the direction we'd come from, and they sounded close to the stairs. "Which room faces the back lawn?"

"One of these." Cass nudged a door with her foot. "Estelle? Are you in there?"

"Cass?" Estelle's muffled voice drifted from farther down the corridor, and all three of us converged on the door.

Aunt Candace already had her Biblio-Witch Inventory in hand and tapped the word *unlock*. The door sprang open, revealing a stunned Aunt Adelaide and Estelle.

"Rory!" Estelle gasped. "Aunt Candace... Cass? What are you doing here?"

"Rescuing you," I told her. "We don't have much time."

"No, we don't." Aunt Candace swerved for the stairs as her sister emerged from the room, a dazed expression on her face.

"Rory? Is Cass here as well?"

"Yeah, she is." True to form, Cass had left the others to make their own way out of the room as she retraced her steps down the corridor to the other staircase. Unfortunately, I heard voices coming from that direction too. We were trapped on both sides.

As I racked my mind for an escape route that didn't involve jumping out of a window, Jet nudged my shoulder. "I can find *her*, partner."

"Evangeline." I shuddered. "Yeah... that might be our only option."

We were far outnumbered. I was sure we must be close to the half-hour time limit Evangeline had given us, but did we have long enough to escape alive?

Cass reached into her pocket then cursed. "Dammit. I forgot to move my firedust over from my cloak pocket."

"Firedust?" I reached into my own bag and then shook my head. "No... we can't use that in here. It's too dangerous."

"Up to you." She tensed at the distinct sound of footsteps on the stairs. "Does everyone have their wands?"

"No, they confiscated them," said Estelle. "I think they put them in one of the other rooms..."

Cass swore and began opening doors, while the others rushed over to help. I, meanwhile, dug into my shoulder bag and found the knotted fabric bag containing the firedust I kept on hand for emergencies.

If I'd been Cass, I might have thrown the firedust directly at the vampires climbing the stairs, except that would have blocked our own escape route and might have hurt innocent people in the process. Instead, I checked the open doors and found an elegant bedroom that contained a huge four-poster bed with highly flammable curtains. That would have to do.

Over my shoulder, I spoke to the others. "One of you—Cass—run and tell the vampires there's a fire. Did you find the others' wands?"

"Yes," Estelle answered from behind me. "They're coming."

The footsteps grew louder. With shaking hands, I pulled out a handful of dust and flung it straight at the fancy curtains. Flames sprang into being, while Cass raised her voice and shouted, "Fire!"

An instant later, one of the vampires reached the top of the stairs and recoiled. "Fire!"

The others took up the cry, while panic erupted on the stairs. We ran, seeing vampires and humans alike fleeing in all directions, and charged through the melee. As I'd hoped, the vampires appeared to be more concerned with avoiding the fire than noticing their prisoners' escape. That or they hadn't known. Carlos Verdant himself was nowhere to be seen.

When we reached the corridor to the front door, though, I spotted him in the doorway, gesturing for people to leave. *Argh.*

Backtracking, I urged the others to stop their approach before he saw us. "There's got to be a back exit."

"There is." Cass led the way past the stairs, ignoring the occasional confused glance from someone who'd noticed the two newcomers. Aunt Adelaide and Estelle weren't remotely dressed for a high-class event, but their dishevelled appearances were the least of anyone's concerns, frankly.

We reached the back door without being waylaid, which lay open. On the wide lawn outside stood none other than Evangeline. Two of her fellow vampires flanked her, while more fanned out behind her. *Ah. That's why none of the other vampires were running this way.*

A smile spread across Evangeline's face. "It looks as if I got here just in time, Aurora."

I indicated the house. "Carlos Verdant is the one you want, but I think he's trying to escape through the front door."

"Thank you for that information, Aurora." Her grin widened. "My people will hunt well tonight."

Not for the first time, I was glad she was on our side and not against us.

Jet landed on my shoulder. "We should leave, partner!"

"Agreed," said Aunt Adelaide. "Candace, that means you too."

"Spoilsport." Aunt Candace didn't argue, for a wonder.

Together, we gladly made for the gate leading to the outside world. It was time to go home.

16

My family and I arrived back in Ivory Beach as swiftly as we'd left. When we landed on the library's doorstep, the ordinary sight of tourists and locals alike heading towards the beach was slightly jarring compared to the panic we'd left behind.

Aunt Adelaide reached for the library's door. "I hope nobody tried to steal anything while we were gone."

"So do I, considering we left Sylvester in charge," I remarked. "I didn't even tell Edwin we were leaving, though he might be busy dealing with Patrick. The werewolf you met at the beach, Estelle."

"He has?" Estelle asked. "Oh, you found Jet, then? I'm glad. I shouldn't have sent him to tail Patrick without asking you, but I didn't expect the Founders to show up out of nowhere and ambush us."

"It happened so fast," Aunt Adelaide added. "They were prepared for our magic too."

"*Why* did they take you?" I asked. "What did they plan to do with you?"

"Question us," Estelle said shakily. "I think they wanted

to learn the contents of that book of vampire lore, among other things. We're lucky you showed up when you did."

"Yeah." I stood back as Aunt Adelaide opened the library door, revealing that the entrance was blocked by a giant brick wall that completely cut off access to the lobby.

"State your names and the reason for your visit!" Sylvester's voice echoed from behind the wall.

"It's just us," Aunt Adelaide said. "We're back. Let us in."

"Give me the password, and I shall oblige."

"There isn't a password, Sylvester," Estelle said in an exasperated tone. "All the ones you suggested were too complicated for anyone to remember."

The sound of wings beating came from behind the wall, which promptly vanished, while Sylvester flew back down and landed on the desk.

"About time," he hooted. "I had to resort to talking to that pixie, who is hardly a scintillating conversationalist."

"Nice to see you again too." Estelle gave him a fond smile. "Sorry we left you, Sylvester. What did we miss, Rory?"

Where to start? "We went looking for you and found the guy who killed those two vampires in the process."

Aunt Candace and Cass helped me explain, which was a relief since I was thoroughly worn out after our madcap rescue mission. I did revive some of my energy when an alarmed Xavier showed up midway through my explanation and was met with Sylvester's resistance on the doorstep.

"I can't believe my boss didn't tell me you were leaving." He wrapped me in a hug so tight I could hardly breathe. "He's going to answer for that."

"He said you'd try to talk me out of going to rescue the others," I explained. "And he wouldn't entertain the possibility of you coming with me. I'm sorry."

"I don't blame you, Rory," he said. "It's entirely his fault, and he'd likely have punished me if I'd gone behind his back."

"I'd have used that stone to call you if I'd been backed into a corner." I referred to the magical stone he'd given me that I could use to call him to my side in an emergency. "But there were too many of us on the rescue mission already."

"Hey!" said Aunt Candace indignantly. "If not for me, you'd have never got into that gathering."

"Yeah, talk about ingratitude," said Cass.

"I'm not ungrateful," I said. "Really, I'm glad you both came with me. I just think that bringing the Reaper as well might have been a bit much, especially when Evangeline came with an entire pack of her vampires to clean up the aftermath."

"She did?" Xavier blinked at me. "I suppose that's better than her leaving you to handle it alone."

"She left the rescue mission part to us," I said. "But she wanted to take out the Founders herself. I hope she manages to round them up before they escape. Especially that Carlos Verdant."

"Yeah." Xavier glanced over at Sylvester, who sat smugly atop a bookshelf. "You might have told me that when I came here earlier to find out where everyone went."

"You were too agitated to listen, you restless pestilent," was Sylvester's reply.

"Sylvester." I shook my head at him. "Did he tell you we went to take on the Founders single-handedly, Xavier?"

"Pretty much," he said. "I already knew that vampire who broke into the library was killed in Evangeline's dungeon. Also, when I went to see Edwin, he said he arrested a werewolf. Was he the murderer?"

"No, that was Joseph." I backtracked to explain how Cass

and I had visited Eric and learned that Aunt Adelaide and Estelle had vanished—and that we'd been ambushed by Joseph on the way back.

"He wanted to keep the Founders out of town, but they got in regardless," Aunt Adelaide said. "I assume Evangeline will decide his fate herself."

"Once she's done with those Founders," I added. "I hope she catches Carlos Verdant."

"Agreed." Aunt Candace scowled. "He deserves to have those pointed teeth of his removed one by one."

"That man strikes me as difficult to pin down," Estelle said. "How did you get his address, anyway?"

"Laney." Some of my relief faded. "Evangeline wouldn't let her out of her dungeon, even to help us find you."

"We didn't need her help," said Cass. "If any of the people at the gathering knew her history, we'd have been kicked out on the spot."

Regardless of whether she was right or not, I sincerely hoped that Evangeline would make freeing Laney from the dungeon a priority when she returned from routing the Founders. It was only fair.

~

THE EVENING PASSED without an update from Evangeline, but I hadn't expected one. By the following morning, we'd received the news that Patrick had been slammed with a fine and a short jail sentence for his thievery, while Edwin was all too happy to leave Joseph's punishment up to Evangeline. I had an inkling I'd wrecked any future chances I might have had of working hand in hand with the police, but there were some threats the vampires needed to deal with alone. Especially the Founders.

As the day advanced without any sign of Evangeline, I told myself that I'd wait until sunset before paying her a visit. She might have had a late night yesterday rounding up all the escaped vampires, and we had enough to deal with at the library.

While the book-wyrms hadn't made a return, we had to fend off constant questions from people who'd seen some part or other of yesterday's chaos. You'd think living in a magical town like this one would lead to fewer bizarre rumours, but apparently, the sight of Cass and me publicly levitating an unconscious vampire through the town square had hit the rumour mill, and Estelle's mysterious disappearance at the height of the carnival had sprung up its own legion of tall tales. Typically, Cass remained hidden upstairs and had left the rest of us to explain—or rather had left *me* to explain since I was the only other person who'd been present during Joseph's ambush.

Aunt Candace found this hilarious. "You're going to get a reputation, Rory," she said, having come downstairs and caught the tail end of my attempted explanation to a few awed students. "Everyone will think you brought down the vampire killer single-handedly."

"I didn't," I protested. "Cass helped, and I only knocked him out temporarily. Evangeline will decide whether he lives or dies."

"Still," she said. "I feel I ought to take credit for teaching you that lullaby spell."

"Yes, by knocking me out with it."

"It worked, didn't it?"

I dropped the subject for now, though I knew she intended to fictionalise the previous night's events to put into a future book. I had zero intention of reading that one, but at least it'd be a temporary distraction from pressing me to give her more material from my dad's journal.

It wasn't until my lunch break that I had time to take a leisurely stroll to the beach with Xavier. We amused ourselves trying out the various games around the pier while a cheery Estelle watched. Patrick, she said, had been permanently banned from the carnival and was currently sitting in a cell. He wouldn't be in there for long, but you couldn't have it all.

When Xavier and I walked back to the library, my heart lifted at the very welcome sight of my best friend standing on the doorstep. "Laney."

I ran over and hugged her, and she hugged me back. "I'm so glad you're okay!" she said. "When Evangeline told me you were going to break your family out of the Founders' house, I thought I'd never see you again."

"We got out in one piece," I said. "Are *you* okay? It can't have been fun to be stuck in Evangeline's dungeon."

"I'm fine," she said. "Though I'm glad that Joseph wasn't in a cell anywhere near mine. I always thought he was a creep."

"Did Evangeline tell you he was the killer, then?"

"She missed a lot of details, but your aunt has been filling me in on the rest," she said. "Cass helped you? Seriously?"

"Believe it or not, she really came through for us," I said. "Aunt Candace too. Where's Evangeline?"

"After she let me out of my cell, she called a meeting with some of her most trusted vampire advisors," she said. "If I didn't know better, I'd say they're about to declare war on the Founders."

My heart lurched. I should have known better than to think we'd get a reprieve for long, but with Laney free and my family back at my side, everything seemed brighter despite the clouds on the horizon.

When we returned to the library, Laney went for a well-deserved nap, while Xavier stayed to help me tidy the various books that had got knocked out of place during Sylvester's security-driven rearrangement of the downstairs floor the previous day. Aunt Candace and Cass seemed to have decided they'd done enough good deeds for one week, so Aunt Adelaide was glad for the extra help.

As the library was closing for the night, I was in the middle of returning the last books to their shelves when the sound of wings fluttering signalled my familiar's arrival.

Jet flew across the library, clutching a piece of folded-up paper in his claws. "This was on the doorstep, partner!"

I frowned and took the letter from him. The words were written in an unfamiliar spiked handwriting, but they turned my blood to water.

Aurora,

Am I correct in assuming that you were behind the recent events at Carlos Verdant's house? If so, that was terribly bold of you, and I'm intrigued to see what you do next.

MV.

MV. Mortimer Vale. Had to be. Which meant he knew that we'd infiltrated Carlos Verdant's home. Who had told him? How much else did he know? Questions burst into my skull, and the paper trembled in my hands.

"What are we going to do, partner?" Jet asked.

I don't know, I thought. *I really don't know.*

"Tell the others," I began. "We gave the Founders a real setback yesterday. It'll take them a while to bounce back, so Evangeline has the upper hand on them for the time being."

"Tell us what?" Estelle stepped out from behind a

nearby shelf. When I showed her the note, her face turned chalk white. "He... how *dare* he?"

"Who?" Aunt Adelaide came over, too, and I passed her the note. As she read it, her expression went completely still. "He wants a fight, does he?"

"He wants us to feel intimidated." I raised my head. "He wants me to know he has someone bringing information in from the outside."

"He'll stay stuck in that cell of his, as long as we have anything to do with it," said Aunt Adelaide. "It's a bluff, Rory. He has no power over you."

I drew in a breath and exhaled to relieve the tightness in my chest. "Right."

I'd drawn his attention, which wasn't a good thing, but I had to remember that I'd dealt the Founders a serious blow in disrupting their gathering and sending one of their most prominent members on the run.

"Exactly," said Estelle. "He picked the losing side, Rory."

"Yeah." New resolve filled my voice. My family and I would ensure that he and his allies would never win against the library. "He and the other Founders will regret making enemies of our family."

ABOUT THE AUTHOR

Elle Adams lives in the middle of England, where she spends most of her time reading an ever-growing mountain of books, planning her next adventure, or writing. Elle's books are humorous mysteries with a paranormal twist, packed with magical mayhem.

She also writes urban and contemporary fantasy novels as Emma L. Adams.

Visit http://www.elleadamsauthor.com/ to find out more about Elle's books.

Made in the USA
Monee, IL
07 May 2025